THE BEYOND SERIES

Beyond LOVE

d. d. marx

Beyond Love

Contributors: Cover Illustration: Michael Fitzpatrick; Graphic Design by Morpheus Blak for Critical Mass Communications; Content Editor: Caroline Tolley; Copy Editor: Tim Jacobs Writing Consultants

ISBN: 978-0-9972481-1-1 paperback
ISBN: 978-0-9972481-4-2 ebook

Printed in the United States of America

To order, go to:
www.ddmarx.com

DEDICATION

In honor of Kevin Tighe.

CHAPTER ONE
(OLIVIA)

"Ladies and gentlemen, welcome to Flight 1021, non-stop service to Chicago Midway from LAX. If you are just joining us, it will be a full flight today so that "C" on your boarding card stands for—see that middle seat? That's yours. Please step out of the aisle so we can close the doors for an on-time departure," quips the flight attendant.

Ugh. Just what I need—to be sandwiched between two strangers for four hours. Reality is settling in. I'm returning home from an unexpected, amazing whirlwind romance to a mailbox overflowing with bills, and the fact that the life I knew has ceased to exist. For the better, yes, but I put plenty of blood, sweat, and tears into that life and, in one moment, it sunk faster than the Titanic. My thoughts are interrupted by a sweet woman with a big grin in the aisle, holding up two drink coupons.

"I'm willing to share. It looks like you could use one of these."

"Is it that obvious?" I say, laughing.

"Hi, I'm Liza Sanders," she says, getting up from her seat and stepping away from her seat.

"Hi, Liza. I'm Olivia Henry and the second round is on me," I say as I shuffle into my seat and settle in for the journey home. I bend over to shove my duffle bag under the seat and blood rushes to my head, making me dizzy. Finn insisted I have a couple mimosas to calm my nerves before the flight as we said our painful goodbye. I know it's only temporary, but I miss him already. I can't believe I finally met my soulmate and have to leave him behind *so soon*.

"Are you coming or going?" Liza asks.

"It's a long story, so you'll want that drink first. Let's start with you," I respond as the flight attendant continues through the safety instructions, and the captain announces we are next in line for take-off.

"I've been in Los Angeles since Monday for a nursing convention. I live in Cincinnati, but I'm going to Chicago for the weekend to meet a couple of girlfriends for the Journey concert."

"How fun. You're from Cincinnati? I went to the University of Dayton," I reply.

"Really? I'm meeting my cousin in Chicago. She went to Dayton, too."

"No way. This is a long shot, but what's her name?" I ask.

"Alexa Williams."

"*Stop it.* We were sorority sisters—Pi Beta Phi's. She and I met during rush our freshman year. We shared our woes over boys and dragged each other to chapter meetings. What a small world," I respond.

"I'm a Pi Phi, too," she replies, reaching out to give me the secret sister handshake. "And you can ask her yourself. We have an extra ticket to the concert tomorrow night. One of our friends couldn't make it. You're welcome to come with us."

"I would love to. Where are you guys staying?"

"We have a suite at the Sheraton near Navy Pier. You're welcome to stay with us."

"I would offer to have you stay with me, but I left unexpectedly and have been gone for several weeks, so

I will take you up on your room offer for tomorrow night. It will help soften the blow of re-entry. One final escape," I joke.

Four hours have never gone by so fast; we chat the entire way. I tell her about Finn and she fills me in on her life and updates on Alexa. Before we know it, the wheels touch down in Chicago. We exchange information and go our separate ways.

#

I take an Uber back to my condo. It smells musty from being locked up for so long. First order of business is to call Finn to let him know I'm home safe.

"My sexy lassie . . . " he answers.

"Gosh, I miss you so much already, but you *do* know that Lassie is a famous dog, don't you? Maybe we'll work on a different nickname," I say, laughing.

"Aye. How was the trip back?"

"Better than expected. I sat next to a girl on the flight who, as it turns out, is cousins with a good friend of mine from college. We lost touch a few years ago. They live in Cincinnati but are in town for a girls' weekend. They invited me to go with them to the Journey concert tomorrow night."

"Brilliant," he responds.

"I just got home. It's surreal. Since the last time I was here, my life has changed one hundred and eighty degrees." I pace around the condo in a daze. I still have laundry laying around; dishes in the dishwasher. I left for work one morning and was gone for six weeks. *Crazy*.

"Frank has been walking around searching for ye all day," he says.

"Aw, sweet boy. Give him lots of hugs and kisses from me. I swear, I never knew what we were missing out on by not having a dog growing up. He is pure love," I gush.

"We just got back from a walk. Now I should clean up and go into work."

"Okay, tell Frank I'll be back as soon as I can. I'll call the realtor on Monday to get the condo ready to sell. I'm sure my parents will have a lot to say about that on Sunday at my dad's birthday celebration."

"Aye. Get some rest. I'll talk to ye tomorrow," he says as we hang up.

I order take out, shower, and hurl myself into bed. Like every night, I pick up the photo of my best friend Danny and me from my nightstand. It's from the New Year's Eve before he passed away. We both look so happy, carefree, and clueless to the horrific event looming ahead. The photo captures a time when life was simple: free of pain, grief, and loss. I kiss it goodnight. *Thank you for always watching over me. The last few months finally make so much more sense now.*

I wake up to a mild spring day in Chicago, few and far between this time of year. I go for a run along the lake to breathe in the brisk air, getting my heart pumping and blood flowing. I run, which is somewhat of a new sport for me. I hate every single second of it, but it burns the most calories in the shortest period. After all, I am now dating a chef: a delicious specimen of a man named Finn McDaniels whose life is dedicated to delivering heaven on a platter. The first ingredient in every recipe, well, besides love is butter.

Butter is also the primary ingredient in the cottage cheese covering my thighs. It's thirty minutes of pure pain and misery. Every single step consists of me begging Dan to give me strength to go one more foot and not collapse.

When I get back to my place, my first instinct is to call Finn. I must keep reminding myself about the two-hour time change between California and Chicago. He works late at the restaurant he owns in Palm Springs, and I don't want to wake him. He works harder than anyone I know and deserves the little rest he gets. I put some music on and start cleaning. The house feels like a collection of "things." Things that were purchased with money I earned during the unhappiest time in my life. I was making the most money in my career as the marketing director at a pharmaceutical company, Hellyxia, but the corporate culture was the most hostile I've experienced. Nothing about the job ever felt right. The moment I entered their headquarters for the first time I felt unsettled. I dismissed it as me going through a big life change. I convinced myself the discomfort would subside and I would adjust, but that never happened. There really is nothing like intuition. Your soul knows even if you don't. I know now working there was absolutely the single most critical part of my personal journey. It forced me to wake up and stop going through the motions. Stop existing and dig deep to understand what my purpose is in this life; determine what it is I'm *really* supposed to be doing. I'm still figuring it out, but my gut tells me it will be writing. My career imploding was the best thing that ever happened to me. I've never felt such peace or freedom as I did storming out of the Hellyxia conference room after I exposed the executive for the fraud he was. My boss, Doug Hemsworth, stole his deceased best friend's identity, including his lofty degrees and credentials, to get himself the job. *Despicable.*

I make a dent in the dust and grime, speak to Finn, and run a few errands. I get a call from Alexa.

"Can you *believe* it?" I answer.

"No, I cannot but could *not* be more thrilled," she says.

"Me, too. Your cousin Liza is awesome by the way. It's so nice to hear your voice; how are you?"

"I'm great. I can't wait to catch up. What time do you plan to come over?"

"I'm all yours today. I have to shower and can Uber over."

"Well, hurry up. We're in 406," she jokes.

"Can I bring anything? Snacks? Alcohol?"

"Nope. Just yourself. We have a cooler with plenty of everything," she insists.

"Okay, see you in about an hour." I hang up, grab my duffle bag, and start to search for appropriate attire for a Journey concert. I remember "Don't Stop Believing" piping through the speakers of every college party. *Ah, the memories.*

We arrive at the Aragon Ballroom. It's an old, grungy, standing room only music theater built in the twenties where smaller bands play. Mostly trendy, up and coming bands, but they get the occasional hair band and eighties group reunion tour. The venue holds five thousand people. The checkered floors are tacky from the layer of beer that's saturated the floor over the years. We grab a decent spot near the stage. We take turns getting rounds from the bar to save our space. There isn't an opening band, so we don't wait long before Journey takes the stage, playing "Stone In Love." They play for about forty minutes then they play a non-popular song, so Alexa and I make a run for the bathroom. The ladies' room has a line thirty people deep. We give each other one glance and both head toward the men's room that has no line cause when you gotta go, you *gotta go*.

Before we know it, the band plays their second encore, "Don't Stop Believing." As the house lights go up, we shuffle through the crowd toward the exit when a drunk guy throws one arm around Liza and the other around Alexa and says, "Hey ladies, do you know what time it is? It's *intercourse* time." By far, the *best* pick up line I've ever heard.

We head back to the hotel, and I am bound and determined to order Domino's. We're all starving and need to soak up some of the alcohol consumed over the last several hours if we have any hopes of not being hungover in the morning. I step into the bathroom to make the call.

As I re-enter the room, I announce, "You guys are going to *love me* in thirty minutes or less."

"That can only mean one thing. Domino's. Exactly what the doctor ordered," Liza says.

We crack open the final beers of the night when the pizza arrives. We all grab a piece and Alexa yells "*Lava*," her attempt at warning us the pizza was piping hot. *Too late*. I am teeth deep into the slice when hot marinara explodes and removes seven layers of skin on the roof of my mouth.

"How is it physically possible for this pizza to still be seven hundred degrees when it left the oven fifteen minutes ago?" I mumble, grabbing for my beer.

"No idea. Do you remember that pizza place from freshman year at Dayton called Emergency Pizza? They delivered it in an ambulance," Alexa says.

"Yes. I'm pretty sure there was a pizza in my dorm room five out of the seven nights of the week, and why I'm still working off that freshman fifteen," I joke as we lay across our bed full of crumbs.

The rest of the night is fuzzy. What *is* clear? There's nothing better than reconnecting with old friends. The last few weeks have been such an upheaval; I almost forgot who I am. I quit my job then got on the next plane and ran for cover. I escaped to California to stay with my cousin Garrett and his partner in Palm Springs. I wanted to let the dust settle. Then I met *Finn*. The biggest and best surprise of my life. A whirlwind romance, and now I am back in Chicago with mixed emotions. I need to close my current life to start my future one so Finn and I can be together. It's so exciting to think about a new life, but this is where I am rooted, where I grew up, and where I met and lost Dan. It's hard to think about closing this chapter. I'm grateful for this unexpected weekend with these girls. They feel like home. Momentarily taking me back to the fun and innocent days of college where our biggest worry was who we were going to ask to the sorority barn dance or semi-formal. *Carefree days.* They also remind me that no matter how much time or space is between us: our special bond can never be broken.

CHAPTER TWO
(FINN)

Since meeting Liv, I've been neglecting Christine's, my upscale American restaurant. A very welcome, *unexpected* distraction. In fact, I never saw it coming. I thought I was having a tasting with her cousin Garrett for the grand opening of his furniture store, Gin & Tonic, when she appeared. It's been pure happiness ever since. No one is happier for me than Tex-Mex, my business partner Jimmy Bolt. We met while filming a reality show, *Delectable.* I won a head chef position at a prestigious restaurant, Mint, in Las Vegas. He joined me as my sous chef, and we've been partners ever since. When I wanted to put down roots here in America, I chose Palm Springs and opened Christine's. I named it after my late wife Christine. I nicknamed Jimmy Tex-Mex because he's rom Austin, Texas, and his specialty is BBQ and Tex-Mex food. He calls me Scottie, being from Scotland and all.

He's been picking up the slack for the last several weeks while I've been out running around with Liv. When I arrive to the restaurant, I pull him aside.

"Howdy, how can I help ya, partner?" he says, putting his arm around me.

"I want to say thank ye. I know I left ye in the lurch and caused ye pressure," I say when he interrupts.

"We're straight shooters; ain't we, Scottie? We're in this together. I reckon my time will come. Plus, that little lady is quite something. That was no favor; she's your destiny." He pats me on the back as he returns to his prepping station. Tex-Mex is a man of few words, but the words he says are bloody powerful. He's been through his fair share of pain. His twin brother was killed in a farming accident back on their ranch in Dripping Springs, Texas when they were fifteen. He's the first person, outside of family, I told about Christine. I met him on the heels of her death. The reality show began filming only a couple weeks after her funeral. What I haven't shared is the unbreakable connection Christine and I have. I talk to her and ask her to send me signs that she's still with me. Things like birds and rainbows. It's a connection most people wouldn't comprehend, so I keep it to myself.

Liv gave me my spark back. She brought me back to life. It was unexpected and caught me off guard. I dove in head first and Tex-Mex has been so kind and supportive, allowing me space to explore the relationship.

Tex-Mex notices me walking around aimlessly.

"Scottie, if you're lookin' for somethin' to do, I reckon you comb through the stack of resumes I piled on your desk in the back. I put 'em in order of best to worst."

We are in desperate need of a full-time manager to run the day to day. Both Tex-Mex and I get pulled in multiple directions and need someone dedicated to the front of the house.

"Aye. As much as I've disappeared, it's a miracle you haven't boarded up the front door," I joke.

"Naw, I reckon this kitchen is the closest thing to home I've felt in a long time." He reassures me he's in the thick of it with me. And he's right; his time will come, and I will be there for him.

"Once we hire someone, I plan to take a trip back to Europe for a long weekend. Need to close a few things. It's time." I need to clean out the Paris apartment where Christine and I were living. My parents bought it as an investment property for their retirement when I was still living in Scotland. Once I went to culinary school in Paris, it just made sense that I live there. Then I met Christine and, before long, we were married. We stayed until her cancer came back, then packed up and moved to her parents' house in Indiana to pursue a new clinical trial drug, Brcaxia, targeted at women predisposed with the *BRCA1* gene. Her cancer was too far gone so she didn't qualify. I haven't been back to Paris, outside of a quick trip with Liv for my parents' surprise anniversary party. I don't plan to ever forget Christine. She's in a new, permanent, portable place now—my heart. It's time to create new memories with Liv.

We narrow the resumes down to five candidates and arrange their interviews. We're having each candidate meet with the kitchen staff and the event manager. Half the battle is getting all the personalities to mesh. I need to guarantee if Tex-Mex and I cannot be here for some reason that the restaurant will continue to run smoothly. Everyone needs to respect each other. I've worked in kitchens where teams don't gel. It creates tension and leads to chaos, bleeding into the quality of the food and overall service. We have very high standards, so want to create an environment where the team can not only learn but also have fun.

We get through all the candidates in two days. We met with each staff member to gather feedback and the entire team has a hands-down favorite. Luckily, he's our top pick, too. Mickey Herrington starts next week. Impressive background. Moved up to Palm Springs from LA so he has good experience in some high-end restaurants frequented by celebrities. It will take him a bit to get his bearings around here, so I have him shadow me for a week or so before I toss him in. Fortunately, we don't have any major events booked, so he can get familiar with the day to day routine starting with every Sunday morning. Tex-Mex and I meet to go over the weekend to discuss the daily specials for the week and check inventory stock then place our orders. Deliveries arrive on Mondays and Thursdays. We open at four o'clock, so kitchen staff starts at one p.m. to start cutting, dicing, slicing, peeling, arranging, organizing, defrosting, and tenderizing. Once those doors open, our only focus is on the customer and serving them the most delicious meal they've ever tasted.

CHAPTER THREE
(OLIVIA)

We celebrated Dad's sixtieth birthday at my parents' house yesterday. I'll admit; it was nice to see everyone despite the barrage of questions. They are proud of me for my bravery in exposing the Hellyxia scandal. They aren't exactly thrilled that I fell off the planet when I ran to Garrett's, but I am forgiven when I tell them about Finn. Of course, they are overjoyed. I have to wait a bit longer before I drop the bomb that I'm officially moving out west. I will let them relish in my good news for now.

The phone rings and it startles me. I hear my sister Jane's voice almost quivering.

"Liv, don't freak out, but we're at the hospital with Owen,"

"What? Oh my God. Why?"

"He's been throwing up since we got home from the party yesterday. We thought it might be something he ate, but it hasn't stopped so we came to the ER to make sure he isn't dehydrated."

"Is Livey okay? Do you think it's a bug?" Olivia, Livy, is Owen's twin sister.

"No, Livy isn't sick. Mom and Dad came over so she could sleep."

"Is it something serious with Owen?"

"The doctors are now recommending he be transferred to Children's Hospital downtown. They don't know what's wrong, but they want him down there so he can be evaluated and monitored. They're taking him by ambulance."

"Oh dear God. How are you holding up? Because I am *completely freaking out.*"

"I know. Just please meet us over there," she whispers, trying to hold back her emotion. *How can she possibly be so calm?* I am a mess just hearing my beautiful, sweet, and innocent two-year-old nephew is en route to a children's hospital.

"Okay. I'm on my way." I hang up to throw some clothes on and order an Uber.

I plead with Dan. Dan is my best friend from high school who was killed in a car accident. We still have an unbreakable bond. When he passed, I had to find some way to communicate with him. I asked him to send me signs and symbols letting me know he's with me. Things like numbers, feathers, pennies, and songs—specifically "Small Town" by John Mellencamp. He was a huge fan of Mellencamp, and the song lyrics remind me of his short but full and impactful life. I keep Dan on a short leash. I am relentless with my requests but he *always* comes through.

Danny, we have a deal, remember? When the twins were born, I told you I would never get married if you watched over them and kept them safe and healthy. Now I've met Finn, so what? The deal is off? I don't plan to trade one for the other, so don't force me to choose. I need to hear "Small Town" stat. I need to know Owen will be okay.

I sit up front in the Uber so I can control the radio stations. I apologize to the driver but explain the circumstances. Before we hit Lake Shore Drive, I hear "Small Town" playing on XM Radio. Most of the time it even takes me by surprise. I mean, how can Dan time it so perfectly? Exactly when I need it? Sometimes, I think there might have been a special deal with God that allows Dan to pipe it through to my exact location.

I arrive at the hospital and head straight to the information desk. A nurse escorts me back to the emergency room because Jane cleared me prior to my arrival. Everyone is visibly upset. As soon as I see Owen's face, I start crying.

Jane steps out from the room, closes the curtain, and walks me over to the nurse's station out of earshot of Owen.

"Liv, you have to pull it together or you'll scare him."

"I can't help it. How are you so calm?"

"I have to be strong for him," Jane responds.

"What do they think is wrong?" I'm frightened to hear the answer.

"They brought us to the ER to get his vitals while they take care of the paperwork. They're in the process of admitting him now. They think something might be attacking his kidneys."

"What do you mean his *kidneys*? I'm no doctor, but the kidneys are vital organs," I blurt out, trying not to hyperventilate as I pace back and forth in the hallway. That's when a warm feeling overwhelms me, and I feel faint. I realize I'm having a flashback. This is the way it happened with Dan. I got a phone call. I rushed to the hospital and stood in the emergency waiting room, helpless, only to find out he didn't make it.

Dan, please, you need to help him. He's just a baby.

"Liv, sit down." Jane gestures to a couch in the seating area. A nurse, observing my distress, brings over a cup of water.

"They don't think his kidneys are functioning properly. They don't know why. The doctors need to run a series of tests to start ruling things out. Owen will probably be here for a couple days. They want to monitor him and see if whatever it is resolves itself. One theory is that maybe he had a strep infection that wasn't treated. Strep is serious if untreated; it can attack your internal organs."

"So is this . . ." I take a long pause, "*life threatening?*"

"I don't think so, but we need his kidneys to kick in. Get Dan on it."

"He's already all over it. I heard "Small Town" on my way over."

"Oh thank God," she says, finally showing some real emotion.

Everyone in my family uses Dan for special prayer requests. "Small Town" has become the go-to sign from him, indicating that everything will be okay. It's when we don't hear it that we begin to become concerned.

"Do you need me to do anything? Before you answer, know that my preference is to just sit here and stare at him until he goes home," I declare.

"I know. He'll be okay. He's in good hands," she says as she hugs me. *How is it that she is consoling me?* Some support system *I am*.

"Can you stay with Livey overnight? We're going to stay here. We will probably be here for a few days."

"Of course. Whatever you need."

I step outside the hospital to call Finn while we await Owen's room assignment.

"*Finn* . . ." I whimper.

"Bloody hell . . . what is it?" He senses the quiver in my voice.

"It's Owen. He's in the hospital," I say as I burst into tears.

"Bloody hell. Are you okay? How's yer sister holding up?"

"Everyone is okay. I'm the biggest wreck. Shocker. I just can't . . . "

He interrupts, "I know Liv, I know. I'm already sending a special request to Christine to watch over him too."

"Thank you. I have Dan all over it. I heard "Small Town" on my way over in the Uber, which provided some relief. I'm going out to Jane's house to relieve my parents. I'm spending the night with little Livey tonight. By the way, on a happy note, I finally told everyone all about you. They can't wait to meet you," I say, trying to maintain some positivity.

"I wish I could drive over to be with you. Text me when you get to your sister's. Keep me posted."

"I will. By the way, I hate to even say this out loud, but, you know, they say things come in threes, like bad news or worse . . . death. First, it was Owen. I don't even want to think about what the next thing could be."

"Don't even go there. Get some rest. I miss you."

"I miss you, too," I respond, not wanting to let him go. Finn understands because he still gets signs from his late wife, Christine. One of the biggest epiphanies Finn and I have gotten is realizing that Dan and Christine were best friends in college. Christine was Dan's college version of me. He called us his *Hank* and *Frank*. Short for our last names, Olivia Henry and Mary Christine Francis. Finn even *met* Dan. Finn, Christine, and Dan traveled together in Ireland after Christine's graduation. She spent her last semester in Paris on a study abroad program, which is when she met Finn. She stayed to teach English in Paris and married Finn. Christine and Dan lost touch shortly after the trip. They were both busy starting their next chapter and living on separate continents, so Christine never knew about Dan's passing. We put all the pieces together when I saw a photo of Christine at his parents' thirty-fifth wedding anniversary in Scotland. We're convinced they're together on the other side and are responsible for our fateful meeting. I'm so grateful. I can't remember life without Finn in it. I don't know what I would do without him. He's my best friend.

I grab a bag from my condo and drive straight to the cemetery before Jane's. I rest my head on his gravestone and plead.

Danny, please take care of our boy. Please.

My parents are glad to get a break. They love the twins, but they are a handful at this age. They are almost three, and their endearing personalities are taking shape. Livey is still napping, but I have my computer with me. I need to occupy my mind if I can't be with Owen. The one thing that relieves my anxiety is writing. I've been working on my screenplay, *The Man Guide*. It's freeing. I write to escape.

Livey is so excited to see me when she wakes up, which cheers me up. She is the perfect distraction. I decide to take her to one of those kiddie pizza places to run around for a bit and tucker her out some more so she'll sleep tonight. I put the car seat in my car, load her in, and off we go. I can hear her singing "Old McDonald" in the back. She starts with all the usual—

cow, pig, horse, then I hear, "Old McDonald had a dick, e- i- e- i- o and on his farm, he had some dicks, e- i- .e- i- o."

I interrupt her to make sure I heard her right.

"Livey, honey, what did you just say? What does Old McDonald have?"

"He has dicks . . . " she says in her innocent voice.

"Did you mean *ducks*, sweetie?" I look at her through the rearview mirror.

"No," she responds.

"Then you meant *chicks?*" I say, trying to redirect her choice.

"Nooo, *dicks* . . . like Grandpa," she belts out. My dad's name is Richard. He goes by Dick. She must have heard my mom calling him that, which is not only adorable but ten times more hilarious. My mom will be mortified. Growing up, there was never a swear word spoken in our Catholic household. My mom would occasionally drop a "Jesus, Mary, and Joseph" reference, but I thought they were distant cousins I hadn't yet met. I'm laughing so hard; tears are streaming down my face.

"Why are you crying, Aunt Liv?" Livey asks.

"I'm not sweetie. These are silly tears," I reply.

This is the comic relief I need. They are so innocent. Full of love and joy. How am I *ever* going to move away from these sweet babies?

CHAPTER FOUR
(FINN)

The house seems so lonely with Liv gone. Even Frank, my rescue golden retriever, walks around looking for her. She was here such a short time but is the only thing that made this place feel like home. Frank and I did okay for ourselves before we met Liv. We had a good routine going. I'd get up and take him for a hike in the picturesque hills behind the house. He'd jump into the pool for a quick swim as soon as we got back while I showered and got ready for the restaurant. Nothing feels the same without her here. There is no life in the house without her. I have to see her, so I pack a bag and drive to the restaurant.

"Tex-Mex, bloke, I hate to do this, but I need to take off for a couple weeks. Liv's nephew is in the hospital. She's having a rough go of it, so I want to surprise her. I'm planning to go to Paris in the next couple weeks anyway, so I think I'll just fly through Chicago, spend a day or two with her, and then fly over. Oh, and can you please take Frank? He always loves his vacations at Uncle Tex-Mex's."

"You best be gettin' your wiggle on. Mickey and I have this place covered. I'll grab the pooch on my way home. Now git," he insists.

I'm on the red eye, so I should get to Chicago in the morning just as she's arriving back at the hospital. Before the doors close, I send her a text. I need to get some details out of her so I know where I can find her.

FINN: How are you holding up?

LIV: Okay. Livey was so excited to see me, which really cheered me up. Remind me to tell you about "Old McDonald."

FINN: I wanted to check in.

LIV: I'm ready to crash. I'm beat. So many emotions.

FINN: Understandable. What hospital is Owen in? I want to send some balloons over tomorrow.

LIV: That is so sweet but you don't have to.

FINN: I would really like to.

LIV: You are incredibly thoughtful. He'll be so excited. He's at Lurie Children's Hospital in downtown Chicago. He's in room 813.

FINN: Great. Get some sleep. Text me when you wake up in the morning.

LIV: I will. Good night. XOXOXO.

FINN: Good night. XO.

We are a bit delayed taking off, which works out great because it gets me into Chicago a bit later than I was expecting, so I have less time to kill. As I arrive at baggage claim, my phone chirps.

LIV: Morning

FINN: Morning, sweetness. How did you sleep?

LIV: I slept like a rock. I needed it. I got Livey dressed and fed. My parents relieved me, so I'm on my way down to the hospital.

FINN: How far away is it from where you are?

LIV: About an hour with traffic.

FINN: Text me when you get there. Be safe.

LIV: Okay XO.

Perfect timing. The cabbie says it will be about forty-five minutes, so I should arrive ahead of her. I want to catch her in the lobby before she goes up. I'm not even sure they'll let me up in Owen's room since I'm not family. When I arrive, I hit the gift shop to get him a teddy bear and some balloons, then walk over to the information desk to make sure there's only one main entrance. I don't want to miss Liv. I sit on a bench just out of sight in the lobby.

LIV: I just got to the hospital.

FINN: Text me an update. I'm praying for him.

LIV: Thanks. XO.

FINN: XO.

I see her enter the lobby and before she gets to the elevator, I walk up behind her.

"Hank?" She stops dead in her tracks. There are very few people that call her that. It was Dan's nickname for her. She spins around, realizing it's me, and dissolves into tears, falling into my arms.

"What? How? I'm so confused. How are you standing here right now?" she says in disbelief as we step aside from the elevators for more privacy.

"As soon as we hung up last night, I packed a bag, stopped by the restaurant to tell Tex-Mex I would be back in a few weeks, and got a red eye out. I'm actually heading to Paris from here tomorrow to wrap some things up in the flat."

"So soon? I can't believe you're here." She squeezes me tight.

"Aye. I wanted to be here to support you, but the ticket only allowed for a twenty-four-hour layover."

"How did I get so lucky?" she asks.

"I'm the lucky one." I plant a kiss on her sweet lips. I've missed her so much.

"I realize this is not the ideal '*introduce me to the family*' moment. I don't want to step on anyone's toes, so let me know where you want me to wait for you," I say, trying not to overstep any boundaries.

"Absolutely not. They will be touched that you're here. I talked to Jane a little bit ago. She called to talk to Livey. They are waiting on the doctor." She grabs my hand and pulls me back toward the elevator.

"You sure you don't want to go up first, then come back and get me? You really won't hurt my feelings."

"Let's go," she says, determined.

Jane is just as Liv described her, and Owen could not be cuter. It melted my heart to see his reaction when Liv walked in. She greeted him with a big hug and kiss. He completely lit up. He is snuggling with two stuffed animals, a teddy bear and a big, fluffy bunny. He sits up to show her the picture he's been coloring for her, waiting on her arrival. *Get Well* balloons surround his bed, attempting to cover up the sterile hospital room. She is so sweet with him. I see a flash of her being a mom to our kids someday. The best news is he seems to be improving, and his spirits are back.

Her parents brought little Olivia down to see them, so we went out to lunch to give them some time with her. They haven't seen her in a couple days. Liv's mum and da are great. Her da is funny. The circumstances are far from ideal, but I'm so glad I came. Doctors are still monitoring Owen through blood tests, but his kidney function levels are slowly improving, which is positive, but there is no official diagnosis, just watching and waiting.

Liv and I spend several more hours with the family at the hospital, then go back to her condo.

As we arrive, she explains, "I wasn't expecting company, so no judging. Remember, I haven't been here for several weeks."

"Stop worrying. I don't care," I reassure as she unlocks the door.

"I know, but I envisioned a very different visit where I was much more prepared, and I was definitely wearing better underwear," she says with a sexy grin, turning on the light in the hallway. I don't see anything but her. She is so beautiful. God, I've missed her so much.

"Then it's a good thing you won't be needing them, isn't it?" I grab her and pull her on top of me on the couch. "Those are some big windows. Are we going to have an audience?" I tease before getting too adventurous.

"Who cares?" she whispers as she pulls my shirt over my head.

We waste no time. We make love on the couch, in the kitchen, the shower, and on her bed. I need to give her something to think about while I'm gone.

#

"I don't have much food in the house, or I'd offer for you to make me breakfast," she says as she stands naked in front of the fridge. The light hits her silhouette perfectly. She drives me mad.

"Aye. Lucky for you, I pre-ordered some Pea Pod, which will be here in about fifteen minutes. As much as it kills me to say this, I suggest you find a robe before he gets here."

"When did you have time to do that?" she says, then kisses me just before walking back to her room to get dressed.

"I'm a chef. I have special powers. Actually, I ordered it from my phone yesterday when you were in with the doctor."

"What did ya get?" she says as she wraps her arms around my waist from behind.

"Round five will have to wait until after breakfast. I need to get some food in me," I joke.

"I'm trying to get as many in as I can before you go. Do you have to leave? You are by far my condo's best accessory," she says as I make my way around the kitchen. The sun is providing warmth as it shines through the floor to ceiling windows, framing the sprawling views of Lake Michigan and the Chicago skyline. The flat is simple but elegant. It's not overcrowded with furniture. A skill that must run in the family since her cousin Garrett is a genius decorator.

"You have no idea how much I wish I could stay. I want to get everything wrapped up, so I can focus on you and us when you move out to California," I admit as I glance over to see her pouting on the couch.

"What time is your flight, and when do you get back? Any chance you can stop in Chicago again on your return trip?" she inquires as I walk over to the couch.

"My flight is at eight o'clock. I'll be there for a week and maaaybe I can squeeze you in, but we still have ten hours." I pull her up into my arms for a warm embrace. Nothing feels better than being in Liv's arms.

Chapter Five
(OLIVIA)

My text sound wakes me up. Overnight my phone is on vibrate, but since Owen's been sick I want to be accessible at all hours in the event something changes. I grab my phone to see a message from Jane.

JANE: Turn on your TV.

I catapult out of bed and charge to the living room, scrambling for the remote. Splashed over every channel are images of a terrorist attack at the Charles de Gaulle Airport. *The airport in Paris where Finn is landing.* I collapse. *Oh my God, this is number three. No, no, no, no this can't be happening.* I grip my phone.

Ring! Ring! GOD DAMMIT RING! *Dear God. Please. Don't you DARE do this to me, Danny. I will never survive this. Never. I can't do it again.*

I frantically text Finn.

Finn, please tell me you landed safely. I'm watching the news. I need to hear from you as soon as possible. Please, please let me know you're okay.

I lay waiting on the ground, on the verge of vomiting, praying for a response. *Nothing.*

Finn, please, please answer me. Please tell me you're okay. I beg. *Thirty more minutes of silence.*

I try calling, and it goes straight to voicemail. I can't breathe. Everything is moving in slow motion. Since they are still breaking details, I'm changing channels to see if there's any different coverage, but every news outlet is running an endless loop of footage of the bomb going off. Airport security footage of the blast is on every channel, but you can't make out anyone in the crowd or see any damage, just an explosion followed by a plume of smoke. All flights both domestic and international are grounded until they determine if the threat is contained.

I don't know what to do. I feel so helpless. I need to call Mac, Finn's best friend, or someone who can get in touch with him.

Take a *deep* breath. Maybe his battery died or he's still in the air, so his phone is turned off.

I mean, what are the odds of being in a terrorist attack? One in fifty million? Of course Finn is safe. He has to be. There's no other option. What are the chances he was in the area at the exact moment the bombs detonated? I'm sure he hasn't called because service is down in the area with all the chaos.

I am glued to the TV, trying to assess the magnitude of the event. There were two bombers. The explosives went off in the baggage claim area forty-five seconds apart. I'm waiting for the death and injury count to scroll across the screen. CNN reports at least sixty-three people are dead, and at least one hundred more are injured, some severely.

Oh my God. No one even knows to look for him. I'm not even sure he told anyone other than Tex-Mex and me that he was heading to Paris. I need to get in touch with Mac. His parents. I don't have anyone's number. I feel *so* powerless.

I call Garrett, my cousin and soulmate. He has homes in Dana Point and Palm Springs. He introduced me to Finn. They grew close while I was out there after the scandal at Hellyxia. He will be just as devastated by the news. He doesn't know Finn went overseas. I need him to get in touch with Mac or Tex-Mex for me since he is local.

"Morning, sweetie. Are you watching the news; when is this madness going to stop?" Garrett answers as I burst in to tears. "Oh my God, what is it?" he pleads and I can barely get the words out of my mouth.

"It's Finn . . . he flew to Paris overnight and was scheduled to land right around the time the bombs went off."

"Nooooo," he responds in shock.

"And I can't get in touch with him." I howl, sobbing uncontrollably. "No one knows he's there besides Tex-Mex and me. I don't know how to get ahold of anyone."

"I'm getting in my car right now and driving over to the restaurant. I bet Tex-Mex can get us in touch with his friends and family," he says, jumping into action mode to try to provide some level of comfort.

"Garrett, this can't be happening. Please, tell me this is not happening," I cry.

"It's not. He's fine. He forgot his charger. His phone is dead. Or the lines are down. Let's think positive. I mean, what are the chances? Slim to none. I'll call you as soon as I get there," he assures.

"I love you," I say as I hang up and run to the bathroom to be sick. The anxiety is overwhelming.

Garrett finds Tex-Mex who has Mac's phone number. Tex-Mex offers to get a text chain going, but four hours have gone by and still I've heard nothing. No one has heard from Finn. Jane and Red are here with me at my condo, doing everything in their power to comfort me, but it's hopeless. Red is my best friend from high school. She was the only thing that got me through losing Dan, and here we are again. I can barely breathe. I've thrown up half a dozen times. The day has been spent curled up in the fetal position in front of the TV, hoping and praying for any new information. I'm praying to see Finn being interviewed or walking in the crowd somewhere near the coverage when my phone rings.

I gasp, "Oh my God, is it Finn?" I sit up, reaching for the phone.

"It's an unknown number," Red says as she quickly passes me the phone.

"Finn, *Finn* is that you?" I ask desperately.

"Olivia. It's Mac. Finn's friend. Your cousin Garrett asked me to call you," he says.

"Mac, yes, hi," I respond, pretending to have no idea who he is. "Have you heard anything?"

"Naw, but his mum and da are driving down to Paris now," he says. "His mum called the airline, but since the explosion happened in the airport they cannot be certain who, if anyone, was involved from his flight. They only have the manifest stating he was on the flight. Other than that, I don't have any news. It will be tomorrow before they arrive, so we won't know anything until then."

"Please, keep me posted."

"Aye, ye as well," he says.

Distraught, I hang up.

"Any word?" asks Jane.

"No. His parents are driving over from Scotland to try to find him. Red, can you get online and book me on the next available flight to Paris, which is probably days away at this point, but I can't sit here. I'm going over there."

"Get your passport. I'll need to add it for TSA," she says, grabbing my computer and wasting no time.

I scramble to find it and hand it to her.

"Liv . . . " she stumbles.

"*What?* I don't care how much it costs. Just book it," I insist.

"No. It's your passport. It expires in a couple months. They won't let you fly," she says, trying to break the news delicately.

"Oh my God, I forgot. I just made it under the wire on our trip to Scotland for his parents' anniversary party. I planned to renew it now that I'm home but forgot about it. *Why is this happening to me? Now what?* I have to sit in this condo, for God knows how long, desperately awaiting any news. And God forbid its bad news. Then what? I can't even go over there to be with him. This is unbelievable."

I throw my hands up in frustration.

Is this some sort of joke, Dan? Why are you doing this to me? You introduce me to the love of my life then completely rip the rug out from under me. What is wrong with you? This can't be part of God's plan. Part of my plan. He can't be this cruel. I can't do it. I won't do it. God should know. He gave me this heart. He knows I can't do this again. Never again. You and Christine have to be with him. Please. Protect him. Please, please make him be okay.

"Liv . . . come on. You can't do this to yourself. You've been glued to this TV all day. You need to settle yourself down and get some sleep. There's nothing we can do but wait. You haven't eaten anything. Dan and Christine are looking out for him. We'll have answers soon. Jane and I will stay up and wait for any calls. We promise to wake you up the second we hear anything," Red says rubbing my back and nudging me toward my room.

"Dan knows how impatient I am. How much I worry. The unknown is the worst place for me to be."

"You know the other thing about the unknown? It could also be good news. Let's hope and pray for the best. You'll be thinking more clearly after you have some sleep," Red says as she tucks me into bed.

I lay awake for hours, staring at the ceiling and thinking about how Finn and I had made love in this bed less than twenty-four hours ago, and now I don't know if I'll ever see him again. I don't want to live in a world without Finn. I can't. I refuse.

My phone rings early the next morning, and I leap out of bed to answer.

"Mac," I say desperately. "Any news?"

"Naw, nothin'. His mum and da arrived. They're staying at their condo while the authorities try to figure things out. Right now, they are en route to the Red Cross area set up for families to check in and review the list of names of victims taken to various hospitals. We're getting closer. Hang in there. I will say that I've heard they've identified all the deceased and have notified next of kin. His parents haven't received any calls, so that is at least some hopeful news," he says.

"Oh, thank God! Keep me posted as soon as you hear anything," I request.

"Aye."

"Did they find him?" Red asks, sitting up on the couch where she fell asleep.

"No, his parents are on their way to the Red Cross tent to review a list of victims. Mac did say the authorities have identified all the deceased's next of kin and that Finn's parents have not gotten a call to identify his body, so that is at least some encouraging news. Now let's hope when they do find him that he's not seriously injured." I look around. "Where's Jane?"

"She went back to the hospital. They're releasing Owen this morning. Turns out strep is what attacked his kidneys but the blast of antibiotics is working, so he can finish recovering at home."

"Oh, thank God. I was so distracted yesterday that I forgot to even inquire about his status. *How is that possible?* Five days ago, I was a basket case over him. This has been the second worst week of my life. I can't believe Jane stayed over."

"She didn't. She waited until you fell asleep and went back to the hospital to relieve your parents who, by the way, are completely devastated to hear about Finn."

"I thought I introduced them to their new son-in-law. He was only in Chicago for me. He came to support me. He would never have been on that plane if it weren't for me. I won't be able to live with myself. . . " I break down.

"Liv. Stop. You can't go there. You can't continue to live in fear. I know Dan, but he's up there watching out for Finn for you. You have to believe that. Trust him. No one loved you more than Dan. He was so protective of you. He's your own personal guardian angel. He talks to you more than I do, for God's sake." This elicits a brief smile from me. "He would *never* take Finn away from you. You so deserve this happiness. It can't end this way. You have to keep the faith. This is the beginning for you," Red asserts as she makes her way to the kitchen to make us some breakfast.

"I want to believe that with every ounce of my being, but I'm so scared. I've been so closed off from love for years for this exact reason. I let my guard down and let someone in. The perfect complement to me. He's my best friend. He's repaired the huge gaping hole in my heart since losing Dan, and now I don't know if I will ever. . . " I stop as the phone rings.

I quickly answer, "Mac?"

"Liv. I just hung up with Finn's mum. They found him." I drop to my knees in relief.

"He's in a hospital about ten miles from the airport. Based on his injuries, they think he was within a few hundred feet of the blast. He must have been separated from all his things because he didn't have any ID on him. He was unconscious when he arrived, so they didn't have any way to identify him," Mac explains.

"Oh my God. How *bad* is it?"

"He's going to be fine. They think he was knocked out with the impact, but then his body went into shock. They put him in a medically induced coma to keep the swelling down. They've done several brain scans and everything looks fine. So outside of several nasty gashes, three broken ribs, a separated shoulder, a bruised tailbone, and two black eyes, he is expected to make a full recovery. His parents plan to stay with him to nurse him through recovery."

"Oh thank God, Mac. I just couldn't imagine . . ."

"Aye. He had a scare with me once, and I had no idea what I put him through until now. I'll ring you again in the mornin'," he says as we hang up.

Red knows instantly it's good news as I collapse into her arms.

Thank you, Danny. Will you forgive me? I am so sorry I doubted you. I just . . . well, you know. I just couldn't. I couldn't lose you twice. You know I love you, forever.

CHAPTER SIX
(FINN)

Mac is calling my mum every few hours for updates.

"How's he doin'?" Mac inquires.

"Improving. They've stopped the meds, so he should be waking up in a wee bit. We're not sure what to expect. They don't think he'll have any memory issues, but there's no way to know for sure," Mum says.

"Hoping for the best. How's his mug?" Mac asks.

"His face is bruised, battered, and swollen so it looks much worse than it is. It is hard to see, but there's not anythin' life alterin'. There is a candlelight vigil for the victims tonight that we will attend. It's the least we can do."

"Horrific," Mac states.

"Have you chatted with Olivia? Been worried sick. I panicked when I had no way of getting in touch with her. How is she?" Mum asks with a concerned tone.

"Aye. I called her after I spoke to you. She's scared and shaken."

"I can imagine. Poor thing. After everything they've both been through. It's just awful. Please give her our love,"

"Will do. I sent a package to the apartment. It's a new phone so he can video chat with Olivia when he feels up to it. I'm sure he'll be very anxious to get in touch with her. I'll text you her number so you have it," Mac offers.

"That will raise his spirits. We'll keep an eye out."

#

I wake up disoriented. Every muscle in my body aches. My mum and da are at my bedside to fill in the details, so I don't have to relive the gruesome scene on TV, at least not yet. I can't make any sense of it. *How could this have happened? And how did I escape with mere scrapes and bruises?* I know without a shadow of a doubt that Christine and Dan were my ultimate protectors. There is no way I could have survived otherwise. Liv must be worried sick.

My mum said I kept mumbling "Liv" just before I came to. I *must* hear her voice.

"Mum, have you spoken to Liv? Does she know I'm okay?" I say, full of emotion. I can't imagine what she's been through, waiting to hear news.

"Mac has been in touch with her and knows we're here with ye. He shipped a phone to the apartment, so you can video chat with her. I have her number if you want to call from my phone," Mum says.

I dial the number. "Finn?" she answers, softly.

"Liv," I say in a strained voice as I try to get adjusted in bed.

"*Finn*, is it really you?" she cries.

"Aye. My voice is still a bit gruff. I am so sorry . . ." I confess as I hear her dissolve into tears.

"I'm a complete wreck. When I heard the news and couldn't get in touch with you, I thought I would die." She whimpers. "I'm so grateful to hear the sound of your voice."

"Mum and Da are here. I haven't seen any of the footage. Not sure I can wrap my head around it. I was stunned when they told me."

"How do you feel? Are they keeping you comfortable?"

"They have me on powerful pain meds. They expect to release me in the next few days, then I'll stay at the apartment with Mum and Da until I can get around better. I won't be able to work for another six weeks until my ribs heal. As soon as I can get on a plane, I will come and have you nurse me back to health," I say, trying to give both of us something to look forward to.

"I tried to book a flight over the minute I heard the news, but my passport is expired, remember? Of *all* moments. It nearly broke me to know I couldn't be there with you. Consider yourself lucky because I would be a nervous, hovering, doting mess. All clingy and annoying."

"Nothing sounds more glorious. All I want to do is see yer beautiful face. I, on the other hand, am not looking so fancy. This mug, once TV worthy, could win me a role in a horror film. Be glad ye can't see me; ye might break up with me. Not what ye signed up for."

"Oh, *please*. Nothing could ruin that sweet, sexy face. I want to kiss every inch of your body. So, hurry home to me soon. Promise?"

"Promise."

It's been six long weeks of recovery, and I'm still on the mend. Although I didn't break anything, the deep bruises on my ribs, shoulder, and tailbone make any movement a challenge. I can't stand being away from Liv, so I am on a flight landing early evening in Chicago. I hobble through the airport to discover Liv's sweet face waiting anxiously for me just outside security. I can see her tear up the moment our eyes meet.

"Can I hug you?" she says, afraid she's going to hurt me.

"Aye, I want nothing more than to be in those arms," I request as I lean over for an embrace. "Just be gentle," I whisper, never wanting to let her go.

"I plan to wait on you hand and foot. Let's get you home and comfortable." She reaches for my arm to guide me out of the airport. Liv is determined to pamper me and do whatever it takes to expedite my recovery. She gets me settled in at the condo before she shares the good news.

"I have a few updates to share with you. I waited to tell you in person. I wanted to surprise you."

"Aye…?"

"First . . . I've spent the last six weeks writing my manuscript, *The Man Guide*. Without a job and being away from you, I had to find a way to channel my anxiety and nervous energy. Writing is my escape. It helps pass the time and is cathartic."

"That's bloody *fantastic*. Are ye done?" I grab her hand and pull her down for a kiss. "I'm so proud of you, Liv."

"Is it ever really done? This might sound crazy, but I think I was born to do this."

"Naw, not crazy at all. That's how I became a chef. I used to help my mum cook when I was growing up, but it was never work; it was fun. That's the difference between a job and the dream yer passionate about it. Passion is what drives and motivates ye."

"I never thought about it that way. I guess I followed the path set in front of me without question.

Went through the motions. Once my career fell apart, I started looking at things differently. I'm amazed at what all the turmoil has uncovered," she gushes. "Very unexpected . . . like meeting you, *but* the best news is I sold the condo. I close in two weeks." She wraps her arms around me.

"*Brilliant*. Best news I could ever ask for," I declare.

"I know. I even got the full asking price. The last thing I want to talk to you about is more of a question. When is it safe for me to kiss every inch of your body?"

Liv asked everyone to not make a big fuss over her moving. She didn't want a big sendoff; it was bittersweet enough. Her parents had a small BBQ at their house today. I got to meet Red and her friends, Liza and Alexa. They came in from Cincinnati. Jane was there with the twins. This time with a healthy Owen. Liv had a hard time with her goodbyes, especially with the kids. They have such a special bond. She vowed to come back every few months to visit. Liv closed on the condo yesterday, so we will start the five-day drive out to California tomorrow. I won't be able to sit in the car for more than six to eight hours at a time. I'll get too stiff. It's the perfect opportunity for us to reconnect and have a fun road trip. Plus, there is so much of the United States I haven't seen.

We decide on the famous Route 66 to be nostalgic. We stop in small towns in Missouri, Kansas, Oklahoma, and New Mexico: eating in diners off the beaten path, enjoying the sights. Tonight, we are staying in Sedona, Arizona. Tomorrow, we stop at the Grand Canyon then off to our final stop, an overnight with Mac and Jules in Los Angeles. Jules is Mac's wife and Christine's best friend from high school. I can't wait for them to meet Liv.

Liv booked a bed and breakfast in Sedona. We arrive in the middle of the afternoon and drive along the river bed, and stop at the Chapel of the Holy Cross to light candles for Christine and Dan. This area is glorious. I imagine the Grand Canyon is staggering. We check into our bed and breakfast, a private rustic villa called Whispering Pines. The pine walls surround the king-size bed with a natural, wooden bed frame. There is a grand, natural wood fireplace with floor to ceiling river rock, and the bathroom has the best feature—a two-person tub.

"Shall I draw us a bath?" I ask, grabbing her waist and nuzzling her neck.

"Not so fast there, laddie. I have a couple surprises in store before we get into a delicious bubble bath, but it's on the list." She picks up the phone to call the front desk. The bellman arrives at our door with a basket full of goodies. Liv organized a private sunset picnic, and the backdrop couldn't be more stunning. The staff escorts us out to the perfect spot, and Liv arranges the blanket, pillows, and prepares the food. There are several variations of meats, cheeses, fruit, and a bottle of champagne.

"I thought I'd recreate one of our first dates. We never saw the sunset that night, though." She smiles, referencing our night driving down the coast.

"Smashing. Yer so thoughtful," I say, leaning in for a lingering kiss.

"I'd like to propose a toast," she says as she raises her glass. "To *never* scaring the shit out of me again."

"Aye, and you either," I respond, agreeing.

"I mean, if you wanted to break up with me, there were much easier ways," she jokes.

"I don't ever want to leave you again, Liv," I say as a tear rolls down my cheek.

"We've both been through so much. Let's pray this is a fresh start. A beautiful new beginning of only good things." We cuddle up, taking in the amazing scenery. The sun is just about to set behind the red rocks.

"We have faith that Dan and Christine are with us, sending us signs and watching over us. I have no doubt they are the only reason I am sitting here today. I believe they protected me during the attack. I've now seen the footage and the damage. It's a miracle I walked away," I say, grateful for this moment. "Remember how they put me into a medically induced coma when I first arrived at the hospital?"

"Yes," she says, listening intently.

"I'm having flashbacks. The doctors warned me it could happen since my body went into shock. My brain suppressed the event. They said certain things might trigger my memory and images re-surface, helping me to put the pieces of the puzzle back together."

"What? Why didn't you say something sooner?" she asks with concern in her voice.

"It's only happened a couple times, but it's *what* I'm remembering that's startling," I continue. "The flashback is an image of Christine appearing over me just after the bomb went off. She said, 'Believe in me. Everything will be okay.' She hugged me and left."

"Finn, that's incredible," she says, getting emotional. "What did she look like?"

"I can't make out her face or body. It was just a silhouette and hearing her voice. Do you think I'm imagining it? Maybe it was a dream?"

"I believe with everything in my soul that was her. No question. Dan was probably standing right behind her. I have chills running through my entire body," she reveals.

"If you have chills, maybe we should go back so I can get you into that bubble bath." We laugh; confident it is no coincidence.

CHAPTER SEVEN
(OLIVIA)

Finn is restless riding as a passenger, so he offers to drive this final leg. We are listening to Bruce Springsteen, "Glory Days", on XM Radio with the windows rolled down, enjoying the fresh air along the two-lane highway. Most of it is sparse desert with an occasional gas station or diner sighting. You realize just how remote some of these parts of the country are. You wouldn't want to break down out here. I'm trying to take in the scenery and be in the moment, but my mind is racing. Our last stop is an overnight with Mac and Jules, and the apprehension is settling in. This isn't the normal "I'm meeting his best friends for the first-time" nervousness; this is much deeper. I'm *full* of anxiety. Mac and I had a one-night stand. He was my Second City instructor when I took classes in Chicago a few years ago. And I haven't told Finn. I'm scared he will freak out and end things. I'm praying Mac doesn't recognize me. It was one night, and we were *both* drunk. I snuck out in the middle of the night and never saw him or heard from him again. It was a "wham, bam, thank you, ma'am" kind of hookup. My first and only one night stand I might add. *What are the chances? Why couldn't I just win the Powerball?* It would be less pressure. These are the types of things that *only* happen to me.

The closer we get to LA, the more the paranoia sets in. *What if Mac does recognize me? Is our secret going to be outed the minute he opens the door?* I'm praying he doesn't remember anything. He's a big celebrity now. Since his tour with Second City, he's become a well-known writer in Hollywood. He's the head writer for the popular sitcom *Roommates*. I'm sure he had his fair share of one-night stands. I'm just another notch on the bedpost. I mean, I'm good in bed, but I don't think our night was anything magical.

"Liv, are ye okay? Yer quiet this morning." Finn reaches over and grabs my hand. "Are ye daydreaming? Mentally finishing that manuscript?" He smiles.

"I think all the driving is catching up to me, plus you didn't give me much time to sleep last night," I say, trying to be nonchalant. He is sensing my mood. I need to perk up *stat*.

"How's Tex-Mex? Is he holding up without you at the restaurant?" I try to inject some new conversation into the ride. "This has been a long stretch without you."

"Aye. Thank the Lord we hired Mickey to manage the day to day. Tex is used to the pressure. As a chef, you have two modes—on and off. The adrenalin keeps you goin'."

"I'm sure he's ready for a reprieve," I comment.

"He'll have to get used to it if we grow the business. We've been tossin' around the idea of opening another restaurant, not in Palm Springs but Texas where Tex has roots."

"That's wonderful. I knew that was the goal, and now is as good a time as any," I say, rubbing the back of his head. "What kind of restaurant?"

"It would be a different concept than Christine's. We're high-end American. We target a more prestigious clientele in Palm Springs. This would be something more appropriate for that region, either BBQ, Tex-Mex, or a combination of both. Tex grew up on a farm near Austin. This is what he knows best. He calls it 'cowboy cuisine'." He laughs.

"If you want assistance putting a business plan together, I'd love to help. I'll be looking to fill my time," I offer.

"I'm counting on it," he says with a smile.

We stop at a rest area for one last break. We are an hour out from LA. Finn gets out to fill up the gas, and I text Garrett.

OLIVIA: *Garrett, talk me off the ledge.*

GARRETT: *Hi sweetie, what's up?*

OLIVIA: *Finn and I are an hour away from Mac's house. This is happening. I'm going to meet him, and I am freaking out.*

GARRETT: *Do you want to make a bet?*

OLIVIA: *On what?*

GARRETT: *Let's bet $500 he doesn't recognize you.*

OLIVIA: *As much as I want that statement to be insulting, I pray to God you're right. You're on. Now, can you tell my stomach that? I'm a wreck, and the last thing I need is explosive diarrhea when I get there.*

GARRETT: *Too much information. Class it up a bit. Would you, Liv?*

OLIVIA: LOL. *Love you!*

GARRETT: *Remember—keep it in* THE VAULT. *Keep me posted.*

It's surreal to think this is happening. Six months ago, I was leading a completely different life. I was on top of my game, marketing a new, cutting-edge breast cancer clinical drug for a pharmaceutical company, pretending I was making a difference. Now, I have Finn; I'm throwing myself into writing and throwing caution to the wind by not having a plan. I don't know what's next. It's part of the excitement, anxiety, and *terror*. I'm trusting this path I'm on and letting the universe, and Dan, guide me to whatever happens next. I just don't want to throw a monkey wrench into things with my drama. *Deep breaths*.

We pull up to their gate. Finn calls up to the house for them to buzz us in as I peer out the window in awe.

"You could have warned me," I snarl at Finn.

"'Bout what?"

"About the fact that they are *kazillionaires*. This is the biggest house, or should I say castle, I've *ever* seen. I guess the romantic comedy writing business pays well." Behind the gate is a sprawling Mediterranean estate. Spotlights illuminate the palm trees lining the grounds. The curved, cobblestone driveway leads you up to a grand entrance. The front door must be thirty feet tall, framed with majestic columns. I feel like I'm pulling up to a five-star resort.

"You won't meet two kinder and down to earth people. Don't let the surroundings fool you," he insists.

"I am not judging. I'm thinking about how we're going to ask for a key to the *casita* for our weekend visits," I joke as we continue up the long, winding driveway. We see Jules come running from the house, waving her hands in excitement. Finn rolls down the window to greet her as she leans in to give him a kiss on the cheek.

"Olivia, I can't contain myself any longer. We've heard so much about you," she says as she runs over to my side of the car. *God, I hope she still feels that way in two minutes when I meet Mac, who is right on her heels.* I brace myself and get out of the car as she reaches out for a hug.

"I'm a hugger; I hope that's okay?" she asks mid-hug.

"Of course, me too. *So* great to meet you," I respond as I see Mac approaching out of the corner of my eye.

"Aye lassie, we've heard so much 'bout ye. Pleasure to meet ye," Mac says as I study him to see if he has any mental triggers going off. *Annnnnnnnnnd we're clear.* Well, he is an actor, so maybe he's good at hiding his facial expressions. Either way, I'm going to go with . . . he doesn't remember me. I take a giant sigh of relief, and the urge to vomit subsides. They lead us into the house. The grand foyer has views straight through to the luxurious backyard. Jules directs us up the marble staircase, escorting us to our bedroom, which feels like the private wing in a castle. It's a magnificent home. I'm guessing ten thousand square feet. I've never seen anything like it so have nothing to compare it to. I'm stunned by all the lavish decor. All I can think is *wait until Garrett gets his eyes on this place.*

We settle in and I send Garrett a quick update.

OLIVIA: Coast is clear!

GARRETT: *Feel free to wire me that $500.*

Finn insists on making dinner. He's itching to get back into the kitchen. This is the perfect opportunity to test his stamina. See how long he can be on his feet and determine the range of motion in his shoulder. Mac and Jules' kitchen is nicer than most restaurants I've been to. The spectacular view through the wall of floor to ceiling windows highlights the pool and outdoor seating area surrounded by palm trees. So lush.

Finn makes us homemade parmesan chicken over linguini pasta. Wine is flowing. I already feel like I've known these two my whole life. They are so welcoming. They remind me of Red and Dan. Similar stories and antics. I'm still trying to suppress the Mac guilt, but the twinge is still lingering. We drink our dessert.

"Finn, remember sneaking out of our dormitory at rugby camp, breaking into the maintenance shed, loading the chalk into the spreader, and decorating the field into the shape of a naked woman?" Jules rolls her eyes after hearing the story for the millionth time.

"Aye, or what about your mum finding that beer funnel in your bedroom crawl space? She called your da, suspecting you were involved in some secret wine distilling business," Finn adds, barely able to contain himself. "Liv, at parties in secondary school, we used to shave one eyebrow off the first person to pass out."

"That's funny. We used to mark people's faces with permanent black markers. It would take *days* to fade away," I add.

"Liv, what are some of your high school stories? I've heard these a million times," Jules says, trying to shift the focus to something other than Mac and Finn's bromance.

"We did a lot of the same stuff. One time I was at a party: the parents were home, but we were in the basement unattended with a cabinet full of liquor. We didn't have any mixers, so we were drinking straight from the bottle and mixing all sorts of spirits—run, vodka, gin, tequila. I was too nervous to drink anything because my dad was picking us up. I didn't know if I'd react or if I'd be able to cover it up, so I just observed. I was sitting in a back room on a couch when one of the girls stumbled in and sat down next to me. I thought she might pass out, so I was trying to keep an eye on her. Next thing I know; she is projectile puking all over me."

"Groooooss."

"It gets worse. I was wearing a turtleneck and sweater, so another friend offered to take my sweater to the dry cleaner for me so my parents wouldn't be suspicious. The problem was it was a faux turtleneck . . . " I continue when Jules interrupts.

"Noooo, don't tell me you were wearing a DICKEY?" Jules bursts into laughter.

"What's a dickey?" Finn asks getting lost in translation.

"It's a piece of fabric worn underneath a sweater or another layer. It covers the neck, so it gives the illusion of being a turtleneck, but it doesn't have any arms or body to it. It's almost like a neck warmer. It reduces bulk."

"Liv, you're pretty funny," Mac says.

"Well, that's quite the compliment coming from you when you've made a career of it," I say, afraid of what's coming next when I see Finn's face light up.

"I cannot believe I haven't told ye, but Liv also took classes at Second City, but in Chicago. In fact, it was probably right about the same time ye were in New York, Mac. Isn't that crazy?" Finn says as I glance over at Mac and see the lightbulb go off. "In fact, she's taken such a liking to it she began writing her own manuscript. Go on, tell him, Liv," Finn encourages.

SHIT. SHIT. SHIT.

I nervously respond, "Finn, it's not that big of a deal, really. I don't want Mac to think we came here to pitch my idea . . . it's nothing . . ." I grab my plate and walk toward the kitchen. "Anyone need another drink?"

"I'll come and grab a couple more bottles of wine," Mac offers as he follows me into the kitchen.

FUUUUUUUUUUUUUUUUUUUUUUUCK.

As soon as we clear the wall from the dining room, I hear, "Wait, yer *that* Olivia?" Mac asks in shock.

"Have ye told him?" he moans.

"*Hell no.* Are you kidding? Do you think we'd be having dinner here right now?" I whisper, praying Finn and Jules don't walk in. "I was banking on you not remembering me."

"I remember, but that *was* ages ago."

"Listen, we can't talk about this here. Not a word until we come up with a plan," I say. "Deal?"

"Deal," he says as we make our way back in to join them.

"How about a moonlight dip in the pool?" Jules suggests.

"*Brilliant,*" Finn says. "I presume it requires swimming trunks."

"I can lend ye a pair. Come with me, lad," Mac offers.

"I think I might call it a night. Alcohol tends to make me sleepy," I say, trying to avoid any more opportunities for disaster. "Finn, you have fun. It's been a long time since you've seen these guys. Plus, maybe you should get in the hot tub to see if it will help loosen up your muscles." I lean down to kiss him goodnight.

"Are you sure?" Jules says.

"Yes, please stay up as long as you like. Enjoy each other," I say, leaning over to give her a hug.

"Okay, see you in the morning," she says as I make my way up the stairs.

I'm not sure what time Finn came to bed, but he's still in a deep sleep. He needs his rest, so I don't want to wake him, but I also don't want to go down for breakfast without him in case Mac is down there alone. I don't want him to corner me. I grab my phone and head out to the balcony to text Garrett.

OLIVIA: So much for he'll never remember you!

GARRETT: *Oh no! Can you call?*

OLIVIA: ***No, Finn is sleeping right here. I, however, barely slept a wink.***

GARRETT: *What happened?*

OLIVIA: ***How did we forget the most obvious connection? We were barely through dinner, and Finn mentioned I had taken classes at Second City. As soon as I looked at Mac, I saw the lightbulb go off.***

GARRETT: *What did he say?*

OLIVIA: ***He followed me into the kitchen and asked me if I told Finn about us. I told him hell no and said we can't talk about this until we have a plan.***

GARRETT: *What are you going to do?*

OLIVIA: ***Well, for starters, I'm going to stop taking advice from gay men.***

GARRETT: *Well played. Text me when you get back to Finn's.*

I walk back into the room to find Finn stirring. I crawl back into bed to nuzzle him.

"We should probably go downstairs. It's nine o'clock. I don't want to be rude house guests," I say, urging him to get up.

"Last night was bloody fantastic. Ye fit right in," he says as he strokes my back.

"They're so great. Now get up," I demand, as I hop out of bed and go to the bathroom to start the shower.

He shuffles in behind me. "Just thinking of the environment. We should conserve water," he says as he kisses my neck and back.

He is hard to resist, especially with that accent.

We join Mac and Jules in the kitchen. She has a fresh pot of coffee made and a plate full of the most delightful egg puff pastries.

"Morning. Can I make you a cup of coffee, Liv?" Jules asks. "I remember Finn doesn't drink anything with caffeine."

"Oh, no thank you. I'll just have some orange juice," I say, afraid to tell her that I only drink iced coffee. I don't want to seem high maintenance.

"Let's sit outside. It's a beautiful morning," Jules suggests.

I keep trying to ignore the sinking feeling in my gut. It took less than four hours for the scandal to surface. How did I think I was going to get away with *not* telling Finn? Now, it will be ten times worse because I've kept it from him for so long. *Ugh, Garrett. Danny, you have to help me fix this.*

"I have something to share with you guys," Jules starts. "I didn't want to bring it up last night because I didn't want to be Debbie Downer but . . ."

"Oh no, what is it?" Finn asks, his face full of concern.

She starts to well up with tears as she shares, "My brother, Kevin, has been diagnosed with ALS."

"Oh *no*. I am *so* sorry," Finn says as he reaches across to rub her hand, trying to comfort her. "How long has it been going on?"

"He's been having symptoms for a few months. He's seen several doctors and we weren't getting any answers, so we sent him to the Mayo Clinic. They ran a series of tests and determined it was ALS." She wipes her tears. "It's just an awful disease, horrible. No human being should have to suffer like this," she says, getting more and more emotional.

"They've only given him two to five years to live," Mac interjects. "It's a degenerative disease, so he will continue to lose mobility as the disease progresses. His wife is starting a GoFundMe page to raise money to help with all the costs. Of course, we're willing to contribute whatever is necessary, but they want to pursue organic fundraising channels to raise money and create awareness for the cause. The medical equipment alone and the retrofitting of the house will be six figures alone."

"What if we host an ALS fundraiser? I'll open a pop-p restaurant. We can invite some local celebrities. Tex-Mex and I are talking about opening a new restaurant. This would be a perfect test market for a great cause. I know some art dealers; we can gather high-end donations and have a silent auction," Mac says as he springs into action.

"Yeah, I have nothing but time on my hands," I add. "Please, let me help organize this. I know the medical business with my experience in the pharmaceutical industry. I can help navigate all that."

"That would be amazing. Thank you. I used to run a non-profit so know my way around, too. We can do it together," Jules suggests.

Mac chimes in, "Truly, Liv, we are grateful for yer support. This will take a lot of pressure off all of us."

"More importantly, I'm glad to have found a new friend. Finn has been gushing about you for weeks but still didn't seem to do you justice," she declares, giving me a hug.

CHAPTER EIGHT
(FINN)

When I arrive to the restaurant for the first time in over two months, Tex-Mex and the staff welcome me back with a cake. I'm still sore, but nothing feels better than being back. I've missed this place and am anxious to start working again Plus, Tex-Mex is long overdue for a break.

"Tex, can I speak to ye for a second?" I say, walking back toward the office.

"Sure thing, what can I do you for?"

"Effective immediately, you are on a three-week mandatory leave."

"I reckon you gone crazy," he says.

"It's not a discussion, laddie. You've been carrying this place for months with no more than a night's rest. I don't care what ye do or where ye go, but yer not welcome back in this kitchen for three weeks."

"I haven't had that kind of time off since I was fourteen years old," he declares.

"Well, I reckon it's time ye do," I joke, imitating his accent. "Why don't you go home and visit some friends back in Texas? You have lots to fill them in on between the show, Vegas, and now Palm Springs. Plus, I think you should start scouting some places in Texas. We keep talking about expanding. This is a great opportunity to go look for land for a new restaurant. My friend Jules just told me her brother was diagnosed with ALS. I volunteered us to open a pop-up restaurant as a fundraiser. I figure it's the perfect opportunity. We need an excuse to try out our new menu, and they need open mouths that are also willing to open their checkbooks. What do you say?"

"I reckon I best be gettin' back to Drippin' Springs to do some searchin'," he replies.

"That's my boy. Go get 'em. Be back by the weekend of the twenty-first. I'm having a little surprise party for Liv for her birthday," I say. "She's helping Jules and offered to put together a business plan for the new place."

"I reckon your brain was busy while you were laid up."

Business is steady. We are full six nights a week, which is a great problem to have. The staff is gelling and well-versed on the menu, so we don't have as many mistakes coming out of the kitchen. Mickey is working out well, and the team loves him. I decide to have an impromptu gathering after close tonight to give the staff some socializing time. I never want to be one of those owners that doesn't recognize or reward his staff. They are my front line, my brand. I need to make sure I keep them happy.

I have a Mexican food truck set up shop in the parking lot and get some tunes going. I have ulterior motives with the food truck. I'm anxious to see what kind of business this guy does. Part of me thinks if we expand, maybe we should start smaller scale then turn it into a restaurant. There will still be some up-front overhead and start-up costs, especially having to purchase an actual truck, but the beauty of a food truck is it isn't brick and mortar; it's mobile. It's easy to change location or switch up menu items if things aren't working. There are benefits and risks to both, but I think with the popularity of food trucks in the Austin area. Austin is where Tex-Mex has his roots, and where we want to expand next. It would be much less risky. I'd have to make sure the market isn't saturated with our concept. So, while Tex-Mex is off doing his investigation, I plan to do a little recon myself.

The team is loosening up and enjoying themselves. I want them to not only be coworkers but friends. You're at work many more hours than you are at home, so you better like the people you work with. I manage to get some time in with the food truck owner and get some baseline numbers. Sounds like he sells on average two hundred lunches a day so one meal brings in about two grand, which isn't a bad deal. Something I will have Liv investigate further when we start drawing up the business plan.

Liv's busy getting settled in at the house, getting caught up with Garrett, and invited Jules up next week to start the fundraiser planning. I need to re-engage with the restaurant and spend some quality time with my boy, Frank. He probably thought I gave him away, poor guy. I knew Tex-Mex was a great caretaker, but boy am I glad to have my dog back.

On a lull at work, I head over to Gin & Tonic to talk to Garrett. I need some ideas for the surprise party for Liv. She's excited to be in Palm Springs, but I can tell deep down she misses home, especially those twins. I want to give her a little taste of home and thank her for everything she did for me while I was laid up.

"Finn, oh my God. . . " Garrett greets me as I make my way to the back of the store. "Liv was a *d-i-s-a-s-t-e-r*. And who could blame her, I mean, who the fuck gets caught up in a terrorist attack? One in fifty million? What are the odds? You look great by the way; how are you feeling?"

"I feel great, sore but glad to be back in action. Feels good to be back at the restaurant cooking every day, ye know."

"That's great. What can I do for you?" he asks.

"Well, Liv's birthday is coming up, and I want to do something special for her. She's still getting adjusted, plus I want to thank her for being my nursemaid while I was on the injured."

"That would be great. Sure. How can I help?"

"I was thinking something small: less than ten and just more core group, which includes you and Tristan, of course." I continue, "I was thinking of having something at the house. A cocktail party around the pool. What do you think if I try to fly Jane or Red out for the weekend?"

"Liv would looooooove that. I highly doubt Jane will be able to get away with the twins, which is a bummer because it would be so great if she could bring them out. Never gonna happen, though. I think the Red idea is fabulous. Get her out here to check out Liv's new life. She'll love it."

"Perfect. Can I ask you a huuuuuge favor? Can you make all of the arrangements with Red, and I'll give you my credit card to swipe?"

"Done," he says.

"Thank you so much. I have one more favor to call in, but we'll be in touch soon."

On my way back to the restaurant, I call Mac.

"Laddie, it's me,"

"Aye. Long time no talk," he jokes.

"I couldn't ask you the other night with Liv there because I'm trying to arrange this for her birthday. I wanted to see if there's any way you can score me a VIP pass to a concert."

"Depends, who is it?" he asks.

"John Mellencamp in Indianapolis in December?"

"Aye, I know his agent. Let me see what I can do."

"That would be bloody fantastic. Thanks, lad," I say.

"I'll be in touch."

A few days later, he texts me that he was able to score six VIP tickets for a meet and greet with Mellencamp and exclusive access up-front near the stage. She's going to die.

#

There was no sense in keeping the party from Liv since I'd have to come up with an elaborate scheme to get her out of the house. She just thinks it's us, Jules, Mac, Garrett, Tristan, Tex-Mex, and her friend Tracy from Mayne. Tracy is her stylist and now dear friend and confidant. I decked out the pool area to make it look very glamorous for her birthday. I even hung a disco ball and laid down a make-shift dance floor. The real surprise will be Red and then, of course, the Mellencamp tickets. Garrett is picking up Red at the airport.

They will arrive in an hour, so I'm putting the final touches on everything while Liv gets ready. We're having heavy appetizers. I made Philly cheesecake crostini, bacon bourbon balls, baked goat cheese dip,

Cajun shrimp guacamole bites, and pear, brie, and caramelized onion quesadillas. A variety of things, and, of course, endless bottles of booze.

Jules and Mac arrive first. They're staying here along with Red for the weekend. Tracy arrives next followed by Tex-Mex, then finally the guest of honor arrives with Garrett. I sent Liv out to the garage to get some ice, and Red slips in the front door and out onto the patio. Garrett and Tristan say their hellos, and Liv makes them a drink.

"Let's go outside," Garrett says, "I need to check out this pool." As soon as they step onto the patio, Red jumps out.

"Surprise," she shouts.

"Oh my God. What are you doing here?" Liv gushes as she grabs her for a huge hug.

"Finn flew me out. He thought you could use a bit of home for your birthday," Red squeals.

"Finn, get out here. . ." she yells to me in the kitchen.

"Are you surprised?"

"Surprised? This is amazing. Thank you so much. This the best gift," she says, kissing me. "So thoughtful . . . truly."

"Aye, yer welcome. She's yer best friend. Happy to make you happy." I kiss her then head back into the kitchen while she gets Red introduced to everyone, then takes her on a quick tour of the house.

Liv seems so happy. *Good decision.* Now to figure out when to whip out the Mellencamp tickets. Red doesn't know either, so this should be fun.

Everyone is mingling and enjoying themselves. Tex slips into the kitchen to give me an update on his trip back home.

"So, do ye feel refreshed?" I ask.

"I reckon I was in desperate need of some downtime. I didn't even realize it myself. It was great to go home, see friends, and enjoy some eats until I was full as a tick," he jokes.

"Did ye have any time to do some research?" I inquire.

"Sure did. I'm excited. I really think we can start something big down there."

"Brilliant. I'll have Liv come in on Monday, and we'll start the planning," I say. "But right now, I gotta wish my girl a happy birthday. Help me light this cake."

I set everyone up with some sparklers for effect, and I carry out the buttercream lemon cake I made earlier today, loaded with birthday candles, and we sing her happy birthday.

"Okay, Liv, make a wish . . . and make sure you blow them all out at once so it comes true," I joke as she closes her eyes intently to make her wish, then proceeds to blow them all out in one breath.

"Bloody hell. Those are some lungs ye got," I say, leaning in to kiss her.

"Jules, would you do the honor of cutting the cake while I get my present ready?" I say.

"Sure thing," she says, taking the cake cutter from my hands.

I go inside to get the remote for the music. I set it to "Small Town", grab my envelope with the tickets, and head back outside.

"Okay, Liv, you ready?" I ask.

"Yeeeeessssss," she replies.

"Close your eyes and hold out your hands," I request, and she obliges. I hit play on the remote, and "Small Town" comes belting out of the speakers.

She gasps and opens her eyes to the six VIP tickets to the John Mellencamp show.

She stands there, stunned.

"Are these . . ." she stutters, "VIP passes to *meet* John Mellencamp?" she demands.

"Aye, that's exactly what they are," I reply.

"Oh my God, Finn. Thank you." She pauses. "I love you so much," she says as I wrap her up in my arms, and she starts to cry tears full of happiness.

CHAPTER NINE
(OLIVIA)

I spend the next few days settling in. I didn't bring much stuff with me because Finn already has such great taste. I love this place. He told me I can do whatever I want so it feels like ours, but things don't make it feel like home; he does. I like it the way it is. Plus, I have a personal designer less than a few miles away that will happily add whatever touches we want. The best feeling is I don't feel temporary. I'm not living out of a suitcase or running to a boutique to grab an outfit. It's a fresh start, like I belong here. A feeling I haven't had in a *long* time.

Jules is on her way up to stay with us this week, so we can start planning the ALS fundraiser. Between this and helping Finn and Tex-Mex come up with a business plan to expand the business, I'll be busy.

"Hi Liv, thanks for having me," she says.

"Of course, my first house guest, and it's technically not even my home," I joke. I give her a tour of the house and show her to the guest room. It's painted a deep navy blue with custom art on the walls. The art is the only color in the room. The bedding is monochromatic. It's not overly spacious but has a queen bed, a cedar chest at the foot of the bed, and two bedside tables. It does have an attached full bath, so she'll have privacy. The best thing about this place is all the rooms face the pool, so there isn't a bad view.

"You can stay in here with your new roommate, Frank. He will ditch us until you leave."

"I'm glad to have him; aren't I, sweet boy?" She bends over to give him some belly rubs.

"Are you hungry? Can I get you anything?" I ask.

"No, I grabbed something to eat on the road but thanks," she responds.

"Okay, well, go ahead and take a few minutes to freshen up and get settled in. And *please* make yourself at home while you're here. I went to the store this morning, so help yourself to whatever, whenever."

"Thank you and thanks again for offering to help me plan this. It's helping to distract me, at least temporarily," she adds, unpacking her bag.

"Oh please, it's the least I can do. How is Kevin doing?" I inquire, standing in the doorway, trying to give her some space.

"He regresses a little bit each week. It's gradual but excruciating to witness. All I can think about is each time I see him will be the last best day he's going to have. It's never going to get better. My family is heartbroken," she admits starting to get choked up.

"I can't even imagine what all of you are going through," I respond, walking toward her to offer comfort ad a hug.

"I'm sorry . . ." she says.

"Never apologize. We are here for you no matter what," I reply.

"Well, let me get cleaned up and then we can head over to the restaurant," she says, trying to change the subject and compose herself.

"Take your time. Finn will be there all day, so he can intervene if we have any questions,"

"That sounds great."

She meets me in the kitchen a few minutes later, and we leave for the restaurant.

"You've been to the restaurant quite a bit, haven't you?" I ask.

"Not as often as we'd like with Mac's schedule but yes. Mac helped Finn pick out the property, and I come up on occasion. I like to shop at the outlets and get my haircut at Mayne."

"We should stop by and surprise Tracy. Let her know that you're in town, and that I relocated."

"That would be great. Maybe we can have dinner with her one night this week while I'm here."

"Perfect." We make our way in, say our hellos to Finn and Tex-Mex, and settle into the office.

"So, let's start by brainstorming. Finn mentioned that he and Tex-Mex have been thinking of expanding, so this would be the perfect opportunity to provide a test market for their new concept but leverage their fame to draw a crowd. Before we pick a venue, who are you thinking will be the audience?" I ask.

"Well, of course, I'm thinking friends and family, that's obvious, but we want to raise some serious dough, so we need some celebs that have big checkbooks. I think ALS has become much more widely known since that viral ice-bucket challenge a few years ago. It's out there. People understand that it's a truly degenerative disease with no cure or hope," she says, getting emotional.

"I'd be happy to put together some ideas and run them past you, so you don't have to be caught up in the details," I volunteer.

"That is so sweet but no. Planning this is exactly the distraction I need. I feel so powerless," she sighs "I have to contribute, not just for Kevin but for every family out there that doesn't have the resources."

"I understand. I'm not someone who can sit idly by and hope the problem will solve itself. I promise we will make this such a spectacular event that people will be begging for an invitation."

"I cannot tell you how much I appreciate this. Truly," she says. "So, I'm thinking Mac can get his studio connections: his agent, publicist, and their contacts. Maybe Finn can reach out to some of the other chefs he knows locally, in Vegas, and from the reality show."

"Yes, and I don't know if Finn has mentioned my cousin Garrett to you, but he's a local designer. We can tap into all his contacts, too. He's done work for several of the *Real Housewives*. They're always looking for ways to be philanthropic. So, those avenues alone should generate a couple hundred people; don't you think? What would you think if we did *two* events? One here on the West Coast and then another one on the East Coast. Garrett rents a home in the Hamptons every summer. It's about the same time as the summer celebrity golf outing. We can try to tie it in. I think between the two events we can raise close to a million dollars. What do you think?"

"I think that sounds amazing. And you and I both know if we get the right people there, they will be generous with their donations," she adds.

"I agree."

"I was thinking about a silent auction. We can get some high-end donations."

"Garrett has endless contacts in the art and design space. We can leverage Finn's chef contacts and come up with some great items."

"Terrific. So where do you think we should host it?" she asks.

"Finn says you can have it anywhere. It doesn't even have to be a restaurant; they could take over an existing restaurant and change the menu, but I think we should host it at Christine's. We have the space and guests would associate the new menu with Finn and Tex-Mex. We'll make it an exclusive event then maybe do a surprise bonus day for the public to try the new menu and donate all the proceeds. Oh, I know, let's have it on New Year's Eve. We're normally closed on New Year's Day, so it would be the perfect opportunity to get people in," I suggest. "In the Hamptons, we can switch it up and have it somewhere like the polo grounds to take advantage of the surroundings."

"Wow, you are *amazing* at this," she gushes.

"Aw, thanks. I think in another life I was an event planner. Something I would love to do if there was money in it but fun to do regardless."

"Speaking of amazing, Mac wants me to invite you to the studio next week to meet his writing team. We were both impressed to hear that you've been writing, so he wants to show you some of the behind the scenes and have you shadow him for the day."

"Wow. What a generous offer and incredible honor. I don't know what to say . . ." My stomach sinks, remembering that Mac and I need to talk. I'd blocked it all out with the ALS news and planning.

"He said to come on Monday morning because that's when they start with a fresh episode, so you can see the process. He'll text you the address and details on where to meet him."

"Truly, what an amazing opportunity. Please tell him thank you," I say, grateful but skeptical. *Is this a ploy to create a story to cover up our one-night stand?*

I get up early to drive down to the studio. I've been riddled with guilt since the moment Jules mentioned it. I have to face facts and come up with the right approach to address the truth. I can't keep living this lie with Finn. It's eating me alive inside, and this is not how I want to start our future. I love him so much and never want to keep anything from him. I have to come clean so we can move forward without any secrets. It was never my intention to keep this from him, but I was paralyzed with fear. I was afraid he would walk away if he knew the truth, then days, weeks, and months have passed, and now I have to fix it.

I pull up to the studio. It has a gated lot and security provides me with a badge. Once in the building, another guard escorts me up to the eightieth floor to a non-descript conference room, labeled *The Writers' Den. The irony.* The last conference room I was in was at Hellyxia, which should have been labeled *The Lion's Den*, because people rarely made it out alive. This isn't nearly as lush or flashy, but I would choose it every single time because of what goes on in here. This room symbolizes the coming together of creative minds to deliver a momentary escape for millions of people.

Mac arrives first.

"Liv, welcome. I'm so glad ye agreed to come," he says as he enters, greeting me with a hug.

"Hi, Mac. I'm touched; thank you for having me."

"Aye, ye are my best bloke's lass and are helping Jules with the ALS fundraiser. It's the least I can do," he adds.

"About that. . ." I say as he interrupts.

"We'll talk about it afterward," he says as the rest of the team makes their way into the room. Mac introduces me to the group, and they are off to the races. They start by brainstorming and white boarding ideas while passing endless rounds of chips and sour gummy bears. Just the environment I need to be in to further test my will power. *As if dating a chef isn't enough of a temptation.* I'm blown away by what I'm witnessing. I have no idea what goes into the writing, planning, and shooting of *one* episode. I have a newfound, deep respect and appreciation for the entertainment industry. Don't even get me started on *SNL*. What they must go through to produce one show is nothing short of miraculous.

We break for lunch, and Mac and I go back to his trailer to talk.

"Liv, I'm just as shocked at the irony. I mean, what are the chances, *but* I don't think we need to make this a big deal. It was one drunk night, ages ago, and was meaningless. *No offense*."

"I completely agree, but I feel like it's this epic secret between Finn and me. I don't want to keep anything from him. I can't. You're his *best friend*," I state. "The only person I've told is my cousin, and he is with you. He told me to never bring it up, but the guilt is eating me alive. I don't expect you to tell Jules; I know how women are. It would create tension where none is warranted and it *is* ancient history, but I do have to tell Finn. I won't be able to live with myself otherwise. It's not right to keep this from him, and I know he senses something is off."

"Aye, it's yer decision. Don't fret. That *bastard* can't live without ye. I know that fer sure." We go back to meet the group for our afternoon session when he makes an announcement,

"Team, the reason I invited Olivia to come in today is to see this process in action. Turns out she's writing a manuscript. I thought I'd give her the opportunity to pitch her idea to the group to give her some feedback. What do ye say, Liv?" he says as the group looks at me in anticipation.

Caught off guard, a wave of nausea runs through me. These people are *professionals*. I can't just rattle off my idea to a room full of Hollywood experts. I have no experience other than a couple paid Second City classes that I abandoned a few years ago. *I mean, am I even any good at this? What if they laugh me out of the building?*

Sensing my panic, Mac intervenes. "Liv, believe it or not, we've all been where you are. We all started somewhere. We each took a giant leap off that platform, too. This is a safe audience. This is a no judgment zone. You have nothing to lose. Now, come on, pitch us," he encourages.

"Okay . . . well . . . wow, I was *not* expecting this, but I guess . . . here goes." I begin. "I wrote a manuscript loosely based on my life about a girl who loses her best friend at a young age in a car accident. She turns to him seeking advice and guidance, wanting him to lead her to her destiny through signs and symbols from the other side. It's called *The Man Guide*. She is solely focused on dating and trying to find her perfect match. Think of a storyline concept, like the movies *Bruce Almighty* with Jim Carey where he is granted with God's powers, or *The Legend of Bagger Vance* where Will Smith plays Matt Damon's golf caddy who appears from nowhere as a guide. A man she doesn't recognize shows up, out of nowhere, claiming to be her guardian angel. He tries to convince her he is here to help. The only rule is she has to make her own decisions and follow her heart. She rejects the idea and refuses to believe him, but he keeps reappearing. Convinced she can control her own journey; she ignores his advice yet continues to run into dead ends. She keeps going out with the wrong men, taking the wrong jobs, and making decisions based on the life she thinks she wants. Each time she hits a brick wall, he comes back to tell her she's on the wrong path. These are tests to get her to dig deep, to listen, and to let go. His message begins to resonate, and she slowly begins making different choices. She gains so much confidence and happiness through these new decisions because they lead her down a path to fulfilling her own personal goals. In the end, she realizes that she's on a journey to find herself, and once she does, everything else falls into place." I pause, cringing as I wait for their feedback, having no idea what to expect. Without a hesitation or spoken word between them, they collectively stand and begin clapping.

Overwhelmed, I respond, "*Really*? You like it?" I well up with tears in amazement.

"It's *brilliant*," Mac declares as the team nods in agreement.

Danny, this is amazing. Is this really happening?

#

Mac invites me to dinner with him and Jules, but I'm anxious to race home and tell Finn everything that happened today. It will be a bittersweet evening because I plan to tell him about Mac as well. I can't keep this from him any longer. He's at the house when I arrive and greets me with a hug and kiss.

"I missed ye. So anxious to hear how today went." He hands me a glass of wine, gesturing for me to sit down so he can give me his full attention.

"Oh my gosh, where do I start? It exceeded *all* my expectations. What these writers do is nothing short of amazing. It's incredible to see how their minds work, and then to be lucky enough to sit in the room with them and witness it firsthand is a dream come true. We broke for lunch, and when we reconvened, out of nowhere and without giving me a heads up, Mac announces to the group that I wrote a manuscript. He puts me on the spot and tells me to pitch my idea to the team. I almost fainted. I was so nervous, but everyone was so gracious." I pause. "*And they loved* it. I can't believe it. They blew me away . . . they even gave me a standing ovation."

"Liv, that is *bloody fantastic*. I am so proud of you." He pulls me in for a lingering kiss.

I interrupt, "Wait, before we take this any further, there is something else I need to tell you."

"Okay . . ." he says. "What is it?"

"Before I tell you, you *have* to know that it has been my intention all along to tell you. I would never want to hurt you or ever intentionally deceive you . . .ever. A couple days passed, then weeks, and it just got away from me. I was afraid of how you would react so didn't know *how* to tell you. There was never a good time," I say.

"You're scaring me Liv; what is it?" he asks.

I take a deep breath. "So, you know I took classes at Second City?"

"Yes, of course."

"Well, one week we had a special guest instructor teach the class. After class, a bunch of us went out. I was still reeling from the loss of Dan, and I ended up getting pretty drunk."

"Okay," he replies.

"I ended up having my first and only one-night stand. I don't even remember any details. I woke up in the middle of the night and realized what happened and ran out. I never saw him again."

"All right. . . " he says, confused. "I don't understand why yer telling me this now. We both had lives before we met. I didn't expect ye were an angel."

"I know, but it's relevant because of *who* the guest instructor was." I hesitate to take a long pause. "It was *Mac*," I say, cringing, awaiting his response when he stands up and starts walking away from me.

He turns on his heel. "Ye slept with *Mac*?" he blurts out in shock.

"This is why I was so afraid to tell you. I *swear* I don't remember one detail. It was ages ago. We were both in a blackout, and I didn't even think he would remember me. . ."

"Liv, ye *lied* to me. How could ye keep this from me?" he says. "I don't know what to say. . . "

"Just say you forgive me. I swear, I wanted to tell you, but there was never a good time and with everything that's happened . . . then so much time passed I didn't even know how to bring it up."

I beg, "Finn, please say something. I'm so sorry. You have to believe me. . . "

"That's why ye were so quiet on the way to LA. Then you spent the night at his house and never thought that was information I should have. You pretended he was a stranger. We spent five days in the car together. Not once did it occur to ye to mention it?" He's angry.

"First of all, I don't like the way you're speaking to me. Please change your tone. It was never intentional. I was scared . . . for *this* exact reason. Scared that you would totally overreact and shut me out."

"Well, maybe we don't know each other as well as we think we do. If you could keep something like this from me, what else haven't ye told me?" he says, deflated.

"I was protecting you . . . us. It meant *nothing*," I cry.

"This has all been moving so fast. Maybe we should take a breather and slow things down a bit. I need some time to clear my head. I think it's best if you pack some things and . . . go stay with Garrett for a little while," he says in a solemn tone.

"*Finn . . . wait . . . please . . . don't do this*," I plead, reaching for him as he grabs the handle of the sliding glass door to go outside with Frank.

"I'll wait outside to give you some space," he says, and I run to the bathroom to throw up, then collapse on the floor, sobbing. *Danny, please help me. I can't breathe.*

CHAPTER TEN
(FINN)

Christine, what am I doing? Help me. I feel so lost and alone. I pushed Liv away because I'm scared. It took everything I had to move on after losing you. Please help give me strength to move past all my insecurities. I'm full of doubt. I'm afraid to love so deeply again. Can she and I last a lifetime? Am I moving too fast? I thought I was sure. What if she won't take me back now that I've been a total ass? I know you sent me signs. Maybe I'm not ready to move on yet, but I can't fathom losing her, too. Please send me a sign to let me know she truly is the one for me. She is my best friend. I'm hollow without her. How could I be so childish and let my ego take over? I don't know what to do.

"Mornin', Tex," I say as I arrive at the restaurant for the daily prep, barely keeping it together. It's been two weeks since Liv went to stay with Garrett. I haven't seen or talked to her, and it feels like a lifetime. It took every ounce of energy to drag myself out of bed. These are the days I am most grateful for Frank, my beloved rescue golden retriever. No matter what side of the bed I wake up on, he is always there to offer up his unconditional love and kisses. He's an instant mood enhancer. I won't allow myself to spiral and go back to that dark, cold, and isolating place after losing Christine. I *just* dug my way out of it a few months ago.

"Howdy, Scottie, you seem as ornery as a mama bear with a sore teat these days. Care to share?" he observes.

"Can't get anything passed ye, can I?" I retort.

"These ears may be big, but that just means they're good for listening." He gestures for me to take a seat as he walks toward the grill. "I reckon I'll make you some eggs and grits."

"Naw, laddie. . . " I discourage him when he interrupts.

"It ain't a question. It's no trouble; now start talkin'," he replies.

Tex-Mex is a simple man. He looks rough and tough on the exterior, but he'll charm you with his cowboy swagger and his gentle soul. Our friendship is different from mine and Mac's. It's an unspoken brotherhood. It started the day we visited the 9/11 Memorial in New York when we were shooting the reality show. That day he shared losing his twin brother in a farming accident when they were fifteen. He slipped it into the moment like it belonged there. There was no big lead in; he just came out with it and then it was over. I felt like it gave me permission to let my guard down and share what I went through with Christine's death. He was the first stranger I opened up to. Now, I think that day we began shooting *Delectable* was pre-destined.

"I haven't talked to Liv in a couple weeks. . . " I pause. "She told me she had a one-night stand with my Mac. It happened several years ago before I ever knew her, before Mac met Jules. Liv took writing classes at Second City, and Mac was the guest instructor for the day. The class went out for drinks afterward, and one thing lead to another."

"And you're full of piss and vinegar about it?" he responds.

"Aye. I'm not upset about the fact they had sex. I know it was meaningless and neither of them remember it. It's the fact she kept it from me all this time. I never want there to be secrets between us."

"I reckon Liv was scared to tell ya for exactly this reason, and you went and proved her right. So, I'll make this easy for you. There's only one question to answer."

"What's that?" I inquire when Mickey appears.

"Sorry to interrupt, but I just found this on the floor in the office. What do you want me to do with it?" Mickey asks.

"What is it?" I ask when he hands me the necklace. It's the locket necklace I surprised Liv with in Paris. I took her to the famous Love Lock Bridge when we visited after my parent's anniversary party. The bridge is a lovers' tourist attraction. Lovers intertwine locks and adhere them to the bridge, symbolizing their bond. I bought four locks, representing me, Liv, Christine, and Dan to capture our eternal connection. After we threw the locks into the Seine River, I gave Liv a locket necklace to remember the moment. She wears it all the time. It must have fallen off when she was back in the office working with Jules. This is it. This is my sign. *Thank you, love*, I say to Christine.

"Thanks, Mickey. This belongs to Liv. I'll make sure she gets it." I look back at Tex. "You were saying?"

"Can you live without her?" he asks.

"Naw, lad, I can't," I respond, walking to the door.

"Then I reckon you best be making a call," he replies making the next step an easy one.

#

Nervous that he'll even respond, I send a text off to Garrett.

FINN: Garrett.

GARRETT: *Finn, what's up?*

FINN: Working at Gin& Tonic today?

GARRETT: *Yes.*

FINN: Can I come talk to you, but I want to make sure Liv won't be there?

GARRETT: *Yes. She won't be here.*

FINN: Okay, see you soon.

His responses are abrupt, but at least he responded. He is fiercely protective of Liv, so it's possible he hates me right now because of the way I left things with her. I was never expecting to meet Liv. I had been guarded for so long and stayed focused on the restaurant. She came out of nowhere. When she came clean about Mac, my instinct was to shut down. We all make bad decisions we regret. I gave her my whole self and to think she was keeping something and something that big from me: it made me question everything. *Is this moving too quickly? Can I trust her?* I felt exposed and vulnerable and overreacted.

I arrive at the store and Tristan gives me a wink as I make my way to the back to see Garrett.

He's cordial and extends his hand.

"What's up?" Garrett asks.

"First, how is Liv?" I ask.

"She's a train wreck. Barely leaving the house. I've never seen her like this," he admits. "She's met Jules a couple times to continue the planning, but the first real glimmer of hope I've seen is Liv agreeing to meet her girlfriends for the Mellencamp concert in a couple weeks. She hasn't told them about your break. She's really isolated herself."

"Aye. If it makes you feel any better, I'm just as destroyed. This whole thing got blown out of proportion, and it's all my fault."

"Finn, I gotta tell you . . . it meant nothing. She made herself sick over it. She had so much guilt keeping it from you. But you need to know; I told her to bury it and never bring it up. I knew the turmoil and strife it would create, so if you want someone to blame, blame me," he says.

"There's no one to blame. Mac didn't even remember Liv, which is astonishing but also reassuring. No lad wants another lad thinking about his lass, even if it was only once," I admit. "I need to prove to her that I want her in my life forever, so I need to make a statement. That's why I'm here. I want you to help me pick out a ring."

"An *engagement* ring?" he asks with a surprised tone. "What's our budget?" he asks, quickly lightening the mood.

"What's yer cousin worth?" I joke.

"I'll know it when I see it. When do you want to start looking?" he asks.

"I would love to surprise her with it in Indianapolis at the concert. Mellencamp was her and Dan's favorite.

It's the one place that would mean the most to her, and I'd feel like Dan would be giving me his blessing."

"Okay, how can I help?"

"I'll need to strategize with Red, so we can pull it off. I want the perfect ring, so let's get started tomorrow."

"Okay, meet me here at noon. I'll buy lunch en route. I have a couple places in mind. I'll call ahead to let them know we're coming," he offers.

"Brilliant. And don't tell Liv. She'll have to suffer a wee bit longer," I joke, feeling terrible for being the cause of her sadness, but I need to blindside her.

"Never," he says.

I pick Garrett up at the store. We are driving down to Dana Point. We can't risk Liv running into us or tracking Garrett down.

"How the lass?" I ask him as he gets in the car.

"She's okay. She went for a run this morning, which is a first. She suspects nothing."

"Brilliant. This might seem strange, but hear me out. I have my late wife Christine's diamond ring. I would love to find a way to incorporate it into Liv's setting,"

"Dude, don't take this the wrong way, but there is no way you're giving my cousin your dead wife's ring. No disrespect," he says, trying to soften the blow.

"Naw, lad. I meant somehow using the diamonds to surround the main diamond," I explain.

"Negative. Maybe turn into a necklace or a bracelet but not for the ring," he insists.

"Aye. Got it," I say, backing down. Garrett has impeccable taste, so I need to follow his lead on this. He knows what he's doing. He did a perfect job decorating Christine's and Liv trusts him implicitly, so I'll take his advice.

We arrive at a free-standing building in an upscale shopping center. The store owner greets us and takes us off the floor to a back room for some privacy. The small room is covered in gold and marble with two herringbone captain's chairs behind a desk where a gemologist awaits. My hands start to sweat, and I feel a little light-headed with the realization that this is really happening. This is so different from the first time. We were so young. We didn't have any money. I had a family ring, so I never shopped for rings. *Okay, deep breaths.* He already has a dozen rings pulled from inventory to start. They are lined up in a plush black velvet box with gold lining. Garrett interrupts my wandering thoughts.

"Finn, do you have any thoughts on what you're looking for? Has Liv mentioned anything?" he inquires.

"Naw, we've never talked about it. Something simple and elegant. Nothing fussy," I reply.

"Okay, do you mind if I provide some input?" he asks.

"That would be brilliant. It's why yer here."

"I'd recommend a simple round diamond for her. Platinum. Elegant. Something in the fifteen to twenty range," he suggests.

"*Hundred?*" I inquire.

"Thousand," Garrett declares as the gemologist clears his throat and squirms a bit in his chair.

"Laddie, of course I want her to have the best, but I'm sure we can find something in the ten thousand range?" I request.

"I was just trying to get the real number out of you. Yes, we can stay in that range. Twelve tops." He grins, then we settle in to be overwhelmed with the hardcore sales pitch.

Over the next two hours, I learn more than I ever need to know about diamond stones, cut, clarity, and coloring. We settle on a single, 2.5 carat, oval diamond ring with a platinum band. It's glorious. Now to mend things with Mac.

I can't text Jules because she doesn't know about any of this. I'm sure she doesn't suspect anything because Mac and I go months without talking because of our schedules. I check social media to see if I can get a location on where he is. Looks like he's in town in LA. I figure out the rest when I get there.

When I arrive at the studio, I confirm at security that he's still on set. I still have some producer connections from *Delectable*. The crew lets me know he's in the back lot in his trailer in between takes, so I make my way back and knock on the door.

"Aye, come in," he shouts.

I open the door without announcing myself. He stands up, surprised to see me.

"Before you say anything, I want to apologize. I've been acting childish."

"Lad . . " he tries to interject.

"Naw, ye need to hear me out. I want ye to know that this was never about what happened. It was the fact that Liv kept this from me. Her cousin Garrett told me ye didn't even remember her until that night at dinner at the house when ye put two and two together with the Second City reference. I needed time to digest everything but ended up making myself more miserable. I'm a bloody fool. Yer the two most important people in my life, and I don't want to spend another minute without ye."

"Get in here, ye stubborn bastart," he says, pulling me in for a hug. "Have ye patched things up with Liv?" he asks.

"Not yet but I plan to make an impact. I'm going to propose."

"*Brilliant.* Just brilliant. When and how?" he asks, pulling me in for another hug.

"I've been scheming with Garrett and Red—the friend you met at her birthday party. Garrett helped me pick out the ring yesterday. I'm flying in on that girls' weekend to surprise her, which is even more perfect. She will never suspect a thing."

"That's bloody fantastic. Congrats, laddie," he says.

"Don't tell Jules. Ye know how women are," I laugh.

"Mum's the word," he assures.

CHAPTER ELEVEN
(OLIVIA)

"Liv, you can't do this to yourself. You have to get up. You haven't eaten in three days," Garrett moans as he sits on the edge of my bed in the pitch-black guest room.

"I can't," I mutter, curled up in the fetal position.

"Sweetie, you can't stop living your life. He will come around."

"How can you say that? I've been lying to him. I had sex with his best friend and kept it from him for months. I should have told him and dealt with the consequences, but I couldn't bear the thought of losing him. I thought if I got him to fall in love with me, if it did come out, that he would have to find it in his heart to forgive me." I sob. "I've ruined everything *and* on top of it, I can't find the necklace he gave to me in Paris. I never take it off, ever. It must have fallen off. That's *a sign*. A sign that I've lost him forever."

"Listen to me. It happened once. Long before you ever met Finn. You said it yourself: it was meaningless. You don't remember it. You were going through a hard time, you had too much to drink, and it happened. You never saw or talked to him again. It could have been *anyone*," Garrett reminds me.

"Yes, it could have been *anyone*, but it was *Mac*," I wail.

"How is Jules handling it?" he inquires, stroking my hair and attempting to comfort me, which is not only ironic but funny. There is no question; he will go to the ends of the earth for me, but he's not a warm and fuzzy, cuddly guy. He's more matter of fact. He believes in tough love. Tristan is the soft, sensitive one, but he's down in Dana Point running their store *Cotton* while Garrett tries to piece me back together and manage Gin & Tonic. The role of being a shoulder to cry on is wearing on him; I can tell.

"She doesn't know and will never know. We all agree about that. Jules knows all about Mac's playboy past, so there's no sense in involving her, too. It will make all of this ten times worse."

"Honey, this *problem* is the equivalent of a bump on a gnat's ass in the grand scheme of things. I'm over it. Finn will get his shit together, and when he does, he won't want to come back to all of this." He gestures in disgust over my appearance. I'm sprawled across the disheveled bed with sheets rolled into a ball. I'm wearing a pair of frayed boxers and an old Mellencamp t-shirt. My hair is a rat's nest. He continues, "Now, *pull yourself together*. Get your ass up and take a shower, you *stink*. Those are one thousand count Egyptian cotton sheets you're wallowing in. Even though I can get them at little cost, you're abusing your privilege. Oh, and can you call Jane or Red to see if they can field some of your misery? I've reached my limit if it isn't obvious," he continues as he storms out of my room.

And *there* it is. I knew it was coming. He doesn't play the caretaker role well. I must admit: tough love is the jolt I need to at least get out of bed. The problem is I *can't* call Red or Jane because sharing this news makes it that much more real that Finn is gone. He has to come back. *Dan, I will do anything, anything; just please make him come back. I love him so much.*

Over the next several days, I graduate from the deep, dark confines of Garrett's guest room to the sprawling sea of the couch, entering a week-long movie marathon and watching every romantic comedy from the eighties until now. Complementing my tissues and tears are small pints of ice cream, and I'm alternating between frozen pizza and delivery. The only thing keeping my attention is the constant obsessing over my phone to see if there's a text from Finn that I didn't hear, or to ensure I didn't accidentally put my phone on vibrate. Finn has his own ring and text tone in my phone, so I don't get my hopes up every time my phone chimes. I miss his chime more than any other noise I've ever heard. I haven't tried to call or text him. I can't take anymore rejection from him.

I am trying to re-enter the world. I decide to make an appointment at Mayne, the salon and spa in town, to get a little pampering, hoping that will make me feel a little better. I met Tracy the day I had my first date with Finn. She did an emergency overhaul on my hair before my date with Finn. She is the perfect person to help me through this difficult time. I certainly can't talk to Jules about it, and I don't need to give Jane or Red a reason not to like Finn.

I'm getting in the shower to go over to Gin & Tonic to help Garrett for a few hours when I get a text from Red.

RED: Did you book your flight yet?

OLIVIA: What flight?

RED: The flight to Indianapolis for the Mellencamp concert?

Oh, *shit*. I've been so consumed with this Finn stuff that I totally forgot about agreeing to meet the girls. It's only a couple weeks away, but I don't want to go. There is no way I can *fake* having fun when I'm this broken, so I start laying the foundation to bail. I'll just say it's too expensive.

OLIVIA: I am looking at flights, but they are expensive. I'm not sure I can swing it. I'm still not working.

RED: Don't. You. Dare. You promised. This is part of the deal with you moving. You promised us two trips a year. You can't back out of the first one.

I stall.

RED: I just searched on Expedia and found a direct flight. We are picking up the hotel for your birthday since you scored the VIP tickets. I'm not taking no for an answer.

OLIVIA: On my way to Garrett's shop. I'll text you later.

RED: You better or I'll book it for you. Text me later.

#

I am the last appointment at Mayne for the day. Tracy suggests we go out for cocktails once she closes, which is perfect since I'm still avoiding Red. It gives me another excuse, and, I have to admit, it's nice to have a girlfriend out here. She is down to earth, lighthearted, and relatable. She moved across the country, away from everyone and everything she knew, to get a fresh start. I admire her. We arrive at the bar across the parking lot from the salon. It's a quaint wine bar. They get all their wine locally here in California. As you walk in, you are greeted with a wall covered from floor to ceiling with wine. You pick out your wine, and they cork it for you. We grab a booth near the back. There are only two other couples besides us here, but it's a Monday night.

"Start from the beginning," she says, diving right in. I fill her in on the whole story.

"I'm so sorry," she says. "How have you been?"

"A complete wreck. Garrett is ready to disown me. I've barely left his house. It's about as bad as it was when I lost Dan. No, worse because I *finally* opened my heart back up, and now he is gone, too,"

"Why didn't you call me sooner?" she asks.

"I disappeared and shut everyone out. Jane and Red have no idea any of this is going on. In fact, Red contacted me, asking about my flight to Indianapolis for the John Mellencamp concert."

"Oh, that's right, the VIP tickets. Well, that sounds fun, and *exactly* what you need right now."

"I'm not going," I respond.

"What? Liv, you *have* to go."

"I've been avoiding Red like the plague and racking up every excuse in the book."

"You can't stop living your life every time something you don't like happens. Don't get me wrong; I'm not suggesting this is trivial or that you don't have reason to be sad or upset, but you can't just exit life. The people who love you are counting on you. They miss you. You owe it to them, even if you're not doing it for yourself." She signals the waitress for another bottle. "I hope you don't think I'm being harsh, but this *too* shall pass. I'm willing to bet you money he will be back much sooner than you think. Won't you be mad when you realize you gave up the opportunity to spend time with your girlfriends to sit around and mope? You're a strong woman, Liv. Don't let this break you."

Wow. She's right. I haven't known her all that long, but she is a wise woman. *Dan, did you put her up to this, or was it Garrett?*

CHAPTER TWELVE
(FINN)

"Red?" I say as she answers.

"Yes."

"Hi. It's Finn." I'm grateful Olivia hasn't shared the news of our recent break. I doubt I'd be high on her list of friends now.

"Oh, *hii*, Finn. How are you?"

"Brilliant, thanks. I'm callin' ye cause I need your help with something special."

"Ohhh okay, what is it?" she inquires.

"Well, I know yer gettin' together in a couple weeks for the Mellencamp concert."

"Yes, we're so excited. Thank you again for the VIP tickets. We can't wait." she responds.

"I hope you don't mind if I crash yer party, but I plan to add another layer. I want to fly in to surprise her, so I can propose," I reveal as Red shrieks.

"*Really?* I'm gonna cry. That's amazing. She'll be floored. Do you think she has any idea?" she asks with emotion in her voice.

"Naw, Garrett's been helping me scheme. He helped me pick out the ring, but he's running interference with Liv so she doesn't suspect anything. That's why I need you in on this too, so we can coordinate. I want her to be *bloody astonished*," I add.

"Of course, whatever you need. No problem," she says, gushing with excitement.

"First, I have to make sure I'm not on her flight," I joke. "So, can you please forward me her itinerary, where you plan to stay, who all is coming . . . you know, the essentials. I'll plan to stay at the same hotel but will steer clear until after the surprise. Mac contacted the venue to arrange a private room at the stadium prior to Mellencamp's event, so we can disguise it all under the pretense of the meet and greet."

"This is so great," she says, squealing. "I'll have to fill in the other girls so we can keep the same story. Jane, Liza, and Alexa are all coming, and we're staying at the Westin downtown. My husband is an executive with them, so he was able to get us the presidential suite for the weekend."

"Bloody hell. She won't want to stay with me then," I joke. "I'll be flying in the day before to take care of some last-minute details but will be in touch soon."

"Sounds good. I'm *so excited*."

"Thanks so much for your help. See you in a couple weeks."

Now that I've made amends with Mac, next up is a much overdue visit to Christine's parents. I haven't seen them since the funeral. It's not that I'm avoiding it; I haven't had the opportunity until now. This is the perfect time. I have some of her keepsakes from Paris to give them. She's buried in their small town. When she started deteriorating due to her cancer, we packed up to come and stay with her parents for the final few months. We hoped we might have one final shot at a clinical trial, but it was too late. I wasn't about to take her away from her family forever and bury her in Paris. Christine didn't want to be cremated, so we made arrangements for her to be buried alongside her parents. They assumed I was young and would marry again. It made sense at the time. She is always with me in my heart. I don't need a gravesite to visit, but her parents do. I think they still go almost every week.

Ultimately, the decision was an easy one. Paris wouldn't be the same without her, and I probably wouldn't stay. Plus, the plan was for my parents to retire in that flat. I was only going to live there during culinary school. Then I met Christine, we fell in love and got married. My mum and da let us continue our lives there. Then when she passed, they told me to take the time I need to close everything up. I just brought back the rest of her things.

I fly into Indianapolis the Thursday morning before the concert and rent a car. I drive the hour trip to Seymour, Indiana.

Barb and Denny have lunch waiting when I arrive.

"Oh Finn, dear, it's so wonderful to see you," she says, embracing me with a lingering hug. I know they consider me the last piece of Christine, so I plan to stay as long as they want me to today.

"Hi, Mrs. Francis . . . I meant Barb, sorry, old habit. I never got used to calling ye by your first names. Just didn't seem proper," I admit "It's splendid to see ye as well."

"I hope you like turkey. I made us some sandwiches. Come on in and sit down. We're anxious to hear all about what's going on with you." She directs me toward the kitchen. Everything is just how I remember it except no hospice furniture. I can't imagine how tough it must have been to watch their child die in the house she grew up in. Memories everywhere. "Can I get you something to drink? Pop? Tea?" she inquires.

"Aye, just some water, thanks," I reply. "I haven't seen ye in some time since ye weren't able to make it out to the restaurant opening. How've ye been?"

"Oh, you know, we're good. Maria and Mark are both doing well. Maria has two kids and Mark has three. We love spending time with the grandkids, watching the boys play soccer and the girls dance. They keep us busy. They said to say hello to you," she comments as she pulls out a few pictures to share.

"Well, please give them my best," I say.

"We certainly will. How are things going with the restaurant?" she asks.

"It's doing really well. Busy. I have a business partner, Jimmy. He was the runner-up from the show. He followed me out to Vegas then we went into Christine's together. The goal is to eventually expand. We hired a full-time manager to handle most of the day to day business to free us up a bit."

"We keep saying we need to get out there for a trip. Maybe next summer." She looks over at Denny for confirmation.

"Yer always welcome, anytime. We'd love to have you. So, I have some of Christine's things I want to give ye." I hand them a box with old family photos, her high school yearbooks, our wedding album, and her jewelry box.

"Oh Finn, are you sure you're willing to part with these?" she says, filling up with emotion.

"Absolutely. I want ye to have them. Trust me, I saved plenty," I assure her.

"Thank you, we haven't been through these photos in ages. We're thrilled to have them back," she says, pulling them close.

"Along those lines, part of the reason I'm here is because of someone I met that had a connection to Christine. Her name is Olivia Henry. I met her in California, and, well, we hit it off and began dating. Turns out she lost her best friend in a car accident not too long before Christine passed, which is how we initially bonded. Here's the insane part. Her best friend was *Dan Sullivan*."

She gasps, "Oh my word, I just got goose bumps all over. I didn't know he passed. That is *just awful*." She looks at Denny. "Did you know?" He shakes his head.

"I know, very tragic. Liv has had a very hard go of it. Ye know how Dan used to call Christine *Frank*?" I ask.

"Yes," she says.

"Did Christine ever talk about Dan's friend from home named Hank?" I inquire.

"Yes, she said he called them his *Hank and Frank*," she replies.

"Well, Olivia Henry *is Hank*," I inform them.

"This is truly unbelievable," she says, attempting to process this information.

"She was Dan's best friend from high school. She and I spoke for weeks about Christine and Dan, our love for them, and the agony we went through. We didn't figure it out until I brought her to my parents' wedding anniversary party in Scotland. There was a wedding photo of Christine and I, and she recognized her," I declare.

"I'm speechless. This is *beyond belief*."

"I know; we feel the same way about it. We feel they had a hand in us finding each other," I say.

"And look at this . . . Liv found the photo album of Christine and Dan from when they traveled in Europe after college." I hand it to her.

"This is just incredible," she says, going through each page in detail.

"This might sound like an odd question, but hear me out. Do you ever feel like Christine is around or trying to communicate with you?"

"Oh my goodness, *all the time*. We see rainbows, butterflies, pennies, feathers . . . you name it, and we've seen it."

"Liv is a big believer in signs and feels like Dan is always communicating with her. In fact, she's convinced he's with Christine on the other side." Barb erupts into tears. "Oh, I am so sorry, I didn't mean to . . ." She puts her hand up to interrupt me while trying to compose herself.

"That . . ." she stutters, "brings me so much peace and comfort. What a gift. Thank you." She gestures for me to stand up to hug her then excuses herself to regain her composure. I watch her as she walks down the hall past the collage of photos of Christine. The floor creaks in this one spot where the wooden floors are worn. When I hear it, all the memories come flooding back of those last few weeks.

"So, how long are you in town?" she asks, when she returns, attempting to change the subject to something more pleasant.

"That's another reason I wanted to stop by. I'm here to meet Olivia. She's meeting her girlfriends in Indianapolis for the John Mellencamp concert. I'm going to surprise her. I plan to propose."

"Oh Finn, that is such terrific news," she says, lighting up in excitement. "We are thrilled for you. Olivia sounds like a perfect match."

"Thank you Barb, I think so, too. I wanted ye to hear the news from me."

"Well, you have our blessing, my dear," she states.

"And I hate to break this up, but I'm hoping to get to the cemetery before it gets dark."

"Of course, of course." She jumps up. "There is just one more thing . . ." she says as she disappears.

When she returns, she hands me a letter. "Christine wrote this note about a month before she passed. She asked that I hold on to it and give it to you, but *insisted* I wait until you had enough time to heal. I never felt right about mailing it without giving you the explanation," she says. "So, now seems like the *right* time." She gives me a kiss on the cheek. "And again, we're just tickled pink about your news. It's so wonderful to see you, Finn. You stay in touch, okay?" she gushes.

"Thank you. I will." I cling to the letter on the way to the car. The envelope smells like their house. It's a blend of vanilla, cinnamon, and lemon.

I arrive to the cemetery just before dusk. I haven't seen the grave with the headstone. It's beautiful. I settle in and start talking to Christine.

"That felt good. The timing was right. There was a reason to visit, and it all fell into place. They seem well. I know yer up there watching over them, but it sounds like they're keeping busy with your nieces and nephews. They bring them a lot of joy, which is wonderful. Oh, and I got yer letter, but I'm going to wait until I see Mac and Jules in a few weeks before I open it. We're celebrating his thirtieth birthday, and I'm hoping maybe ye have a message for them, too."

"So, now on to the elephant in the room. You know why I'm here this weekend. I found her, Christine. You led me to Liv. I know you and Dan had a big hand in that, and for that I am forever grateful. I didn't think I would ever love again. I didn't know I would be capable of loving again after losing ye. I will always love ye. I don't want ye to think because I cleaned out the flat and gave the stuff to yer parents that I'm over it. I'll never be over it, but Liv brings happiness into my life again. She's a bright light. She's sweet and sexy . . . sorry . . . and funny. Ye found the perfect one for me if it can't be ye. I don't want to spend another day without her. Please watch over us and keep us safe, happy, and healthy. I love her and never want this feeling to go away. It took me a lifetime to find it once. To be lucky enough to find it twice is a dream. My only request is I need to know that ye approve. That I have yer blessing. Tell Dan I'm sorry for being such a stubborn bastart and hurtin' Liv. I promise I'll take good care of her heart, forever."

Just as I finish, a butterfly lands on my leg.

"I'll take that as a yes."

CHAPTER THIRTEEN
(OLIVIA)

As much as I'm looking forward to seeing the girls, I dread having to update them on Finn. They have no idea that we're not speaking. I've been praying I would hear from him by now; this ridiculous break would have blown over and be behind us. I'm distraught over how to repair our relationship. I've been avoiding the subject, but I can't mask it any longer. These girls know me far too well.

OLIVIA: Boarded. See you soon.

RED: Have a safe flight. Can't wait to see you. XO.

OLIVIA: Me either. XO.

When I land in Indianapolis, Red and Jane are waiting outside of baggage claim to pick me up. We're meeting Liza and Alexa at the hotel. They're driving in from Cincinnati. Should be a fun weekend. They always keep my spirits up.

"Did Finn drop you off at the airport?" Jane inquires. My heart sinks hearing his name, knowing this is all about to unravel. My goal is to make it to the hotel, so I only have to tell this story once.

"Umm, no, he was working, so Garrett dropped me off." I try to sound cheery. "How was the drive in?" My attempt at changing the subject.

"We hit traffic leaving Chicago, but the rest has been smooth," Jane says.

"So, we're thinking we'll get checked into our rooms, get cleaned up, and then go straight to the VIP meet and greet at the stadium," Red says. "They're having a cocktail reception, so we'll be able to grab food and drinks there. That way we only have to Uber it once. "

"Sounds great," I respond.

"Can you believe you're about to meet Mellencamp?" Jane asks.

"It hasn't sunk in yet, but I'm sure it will be amazing," I gush. *Danny, this isn't the way I ever saw this happening. He's the one icon that reminds me most of you. Not only could I have never dreamed of a moment like this, but I certainly envisioned a much happier occasion.*

Just as I finish my thought, "Small Town" starts playing in the car. Red cranks it up.

"You're joking? Are you playing this on your iPhone?" I say in disbelief.

"Nope. I *swear*. Look at the dashboard. It's playing on the radio," Red insists. "Danny is right here with us, just as it should be." She looks at me through the rearview mirror. I well up with tears. *If she only knew.*

"Don't be sad. Tonight is going to be amazing. One for the books," she states as we pull up to the valet at the hotel. Alexa and Liza are waiting for us in the lobby. Red and Jane know Alexa from visiting me in college. Liza naturally fits right in. We get checked in: We're staying at the Westin. in the presidential suite. I still can't believe this *incredible* gift. *A VIP meet and greet with Mellencamp*. I just wish the circumstances were much, much different. The lobby is crowded with people walking around with badges. There must be a convention in town. The lobby bar is buzzing, and we're all ready to get this party started. A personal butler escorts us to our room. He opens the door and multiple bottles of champagne and a platter overflowing with wine and cheese greet us as we enter. I've only seen rooms like this filmed on a reality show. It has a full blown wet bar and kitchen. A dining room, with seating for ten, adorned by a giant, crystal chandelier. Two sitting rooms with big, white, fluffy couches. There are four bedrooms. Two have two king beds, and two have two queens. All of them have their own spa bathroom with a sprawling walk-in shower and soaking tub. We choose our rooms then gather back in the main seating area.

"Now for the most important thing; what is everyone wearing?" Jane asks as she pops the bubbly.

"I'm planning on the basic concert uniform—skinny jeans, black top, and ankle boots," Alexa answers.

"Sounds about right," Red responds. "We have about forty-five minutes before we need to go over. We don't want to be late."

We turn on some music and the drinks start flowing while everyone primps. I've been able to dodge the Finn questions, so maybe I'll get to enjoy the evening after all. I can fill them in tomorrow. I don't want to sour the mood; it'll drain every ounce of my energy. As far as they know, this is one of the most exciting nights of my life. I'm attempting to keep it that way.

We pile in the Uber, and after a short, eight-minute ride, we arrive at the venue. We have a pass that gains us special access to a private back entrance. We're greeted by security and escorted inside. Now the butterflies are settling in. *I am going to meet John Mellencamp.* I can't wait to tell him all about Danny, and the special meaning and impact his songs have on my life. I hope he's honored to know the impact his music has on his fans. I want him to live up to my expectations. He's an icon to me since his music is so meaningful to me. If he brushes me off, it will be *such* a disappointment.

We're in the bowels of the stadium. There is staff *everywhere.* Motorized carts are racing back and forth as they put the final touches in place for the performance. One of the things I love most about his band is the violinist. The crew is finalizing the stage set-up with all the instruments, along with a large screen backdrop that is projecting old school photos and movies from his early days. We are led to a green room where we will wait our turn to be introduced. We have a cocktail, and before we know it, we're next up. The security guard approaches and tells us to follow him. He directs us to an unassuming door in the main hallway.

"Please wait here, ma'am," he says as he radios to gain permission to let us in. "Okay, you're cleared to enter," he says.

I look at the girls.

"You go first, Liv. This is your night."

I press down on the door handle and open the door. I cannot believe my eyes. I'm expecting to see John Mellencamp, but instead it's Finn dressed in a suit, surrounded by a sea of rose petals. I nearly collapse. I look back at the girls with shock and awe to figure out their role in this scheme. They were *all* in on it. I'm overcome with emotion as he reaches out to embrace me.

"Come here," he says, pulling me in tight, and the stream of tears begins to flow from my eyes.

He pulls back just far enough to look into my eyes.

"God, I've missed ye," he says, kissing me. "I'm *so* sorry. Will ye forgive me?" he whispers into my ear.

"Finn. . ." I whimper, unable to speak as he breaks away to get down on one knee. He reaches into his pocket, and I can hear the gasp from the girls behind me.

"Olivia Henry, I never want to spend another second away from ye. Will ye make me the happiest man in the world . . . will ye marry me?" he asks as tears fill his eyes. My hands begin to shake and I burst into tears.

"There isn't *anything* I want more . . . yes, yes, YES!" I respond as he stands up to put the most beautiful ring I've ever seen on my finger.

"And I believe this is yer's, too," he says, holding up my necklace. "Turn around, I'll put it back where it belongs." He reaches around to clasp it then places a kiss on my neck.

"I thought I lost this . . . and you," I whimper, grabbing his cheeks for a passionate kiss. I feel like no one else in the world exists but us. The girls give us our moment before they approach, screaming and fawning over both of us.

"I cannot *believe* this. What? How? When?" I question as the enormity of the moment settles in. "Does Garrett know about this?"

"Aye, he helped me pick out the ring," Finn says.

"I can't believe he let me suffer. I'm gonna have to have a *chat* with him."

"I asked him not to share, so it's on me," he comments.

"Well, I guess since I am now your fiancée *and* he did such a beautiful job on the ring, I will forgive him," I say with delight.

"We've all known for a few weeks," Jane reveals as she hugs me. "It's been the hardest thing to keep from you. I almost leaked information a dozen different times. I am so glad I didn't ruin it. We couldn't be more thrilled for you."

"Do Mom and Dad know?" I inquire.

"No, that's your news to share."

"The real question is, am I even going to meet John Mellencamp?" I joke as I hear, "Well, I was born in a small town. . ." when he turns the corner. There isn't a dry eye in the room as he introduces himself. We exchange pleasantries, and I tell him Dan's story in the short time I'm allotted. He is so gracious and touched by my story. Two moments forever engraved in my memory.

Danny, you overwhelm me. I love you so much. I can feel you right here with me. Thank you.

Finn joins us in our designated front stage VIP area. We dance in a hot, sweaty, beer spilling mosh pit and belt out every lyric while Mellencamp plays all his classics over the course of next two hours. The girls are still in party mode, so they go out to the bars. Finn and I go back to the hotel for some much-needed alone time. He is flying out tomorrow early afternoon to give me time with the "lassies."

He has champagne waiting and called ahead to have the staff draw a bubble bath surrounded with lit candles and more rose petals as he leads me into the bathroom. I stand there breathless, waiting for his direction. I've been longing for this moment for what feels like forever.

"Don't move," he whispers. His warm breath hits my neck, sending chills down my spine as he retrieves the flutes. He sets the full glasses on the edge of the tub. My body begins to tremble in anticipation.

He brushes his hands on my face, caressing my cheeks and looking deep into my eyes.

"My God, yer beautiful," he says as he leans in for a delicious kiss, his hands exploring. He breaks away and grabs the hem of my shirt, lifting it over my head. I reach for his belt buckle and he pushes my hand away. "No, I want to concentrate on undressing you," he reveals as he shifts behind me. He slowly unbuttons and removes my pants, pulling them past my hips. He begins with a trail of soft kisses from my neck to my shoulders then unbuckles my bra. The fabric sliding down my shoulders then arms as he grazes my nipples with his fingertips, eliciting a moan. I shudder as his hands move gently down to my stomach. I lean my head back to rest on his shoulders, encouraging him to continue. Next, he slips his hand inside the band of my panties urging them down my legs, taking me to the brink. "Now pour yourself into that bathtub . . . I'm *just* getting started," he says, leaving me weak in the knees.

We wake up late morning after a long night of lovemaking. Not wanting to move, I pinch myself to make sure it's all real. Then I glance down and catch the sparkling diamond ring on my finger. *Last night was a dream. I never want it to end.*

"Mornin' gorgeous, or should I say future Mrs. McDaniel's?" He kisses the top of my head while our bodies remain intertwined.

"God, I love the sound of that . . . Olivia McDaniels." I lift my head to his lips for a long kiss. "I don't want you to go," I whimper. "I just got you back."

"Me, either. Yer the best thing that's ever happened to me, Liv. I mean it," he declares.

"I love you so much. I don't know how I survived; truly, I don't. These last several weeks have been the worst of my life. I spent days trying to dissect my feelings to understand why it felt so different. I realized that because of *my actions*, I'd be responsible for you walking away. I would've never forgiven myself," I moan. "You're my best friend."

"I could *never* let you go. I was being stubborn. I overreacted because you kept it from me. I never want secrets between us—ever," he adds. "It kills me to know I've caused you so much pain. I never want to hurt ye. Know that I will continue to choose ye over and over, always and forever."

We make love one last time before we have to say our painful goodbyes. I walk him down to the bell station to see him off in his Uber.

"As soon as I land, I'll go to Garrett's to pick up all yer stuff. Tell him he can finally call that a *guest room*. Ye won't ever be back."

"I miss you already." I pry myself out of his arms.

"Go have fun with yer girls and hurry back to me," he says, giving me one last lingering kiss.

CHAPTER FOURTEEN
(FINN)

Liv's idea of hosting this fundraiser on New Year's Eve was a brilliant one. It's turned into the most sought-after event in Palm Springs. We offered tickets up to our restaurant's capacity, but they were still in demand. We are overflowing into tomorrow, which also includes the public; a perfect way for us to reach a broader audience. Jules and Liv have been working tirelessly to plan, market, and get the word out. They were able to get a large corporate sponsorship from a construction company in the area, adding more money to the pot. Mac, Garrett, and I all pooled our contacts to round up a couple hundred guests. Hopefully, they are all in the giving spirit.

The girls have secured some wonderful auction items, like a helicopter ride to Santa Barbara, a VIP tour in the Monterey and Carmel Wineries, and a Pebble Beach golf experience with a local pro; one of the celebrities from *The Real Housewives of Orange County* offered her home up for a day, and there is a four-day, three-night stay in Malibu. There are some other small, miscellaneous items, like Tracy, from Mayne, donated a spa day for two. Everything helps. We're even donating a group dinner for ten.

The staff is excited with the theme of the new restaurant that we have lovingly titled *Texy-Mexy* after our favorite chef and muse, Jimmy. He's proud of how much the staff has embraced the concept. We had a dry run and made everything on the menu. We had the staff rate items, in order, from their favorite to their least favorite. The instructions were to label the items from one to eight. Not one of them gave a score less than a two on any item. We hope the crowd feels the same way, but we've told each other that, no matter what, this is about raising money. If people love the food too, that's a bonus.

We're three hours from opening when Liv pulls me aside.

"Tracy just texted and said she's bringing in one of her clients that's cute and single. She wants to set her up with Tex. What do you think?" she says.

"I think it's *brilliant*. This fundraiser has really lit a spark in him. I've never seen him this jazzed about anything," I respond.

"Okay, perfect, but do *not* tell him. We'll play it cool and try to let it happen naturally," she says.

"Aye, I don't want him fumblin' all over himself," I agree.

We get back to our duties: she is setting up the front of the house and me prepping in the back.

This will be the real test. We've only staggered guests by a half hour over a three-hour period to give the kitchen a chance to keep up. Even though they've made all the food, it isn't old hat yet.

The first group is here, and everything is going off without a hitch. The girls are making rounds to see what people think of the food, and we're getting rave reviews. Jules' brother Kevin, the guest of honor, is making his way through the dining room, thanking everyone for their support. He is still able to get around with a walker. So far, the most ordered item is the spicy short rib corn bread empanada. I encourage Tex-Mex to take a break. He hasn't sat down all day, and I see Tracy over by the bar with her friend, who is quite cute. I approve on his behalf. Liv intercepts him and I see her making introductions. From the kitchen, I'm watching his body language, and he isn't tensing up, which is a good sign. He seems comfortable and natural. I turn my attention back to the line for a few minutes when Liv makes her way back to give me an update.

"Sooooo, they seem to be hitting it off and with no added encouragement or pressure from either side."

"What's her story?" I ask.

"Believe it or not she's a native from Palm Springs. Grew up here and, wait for it, her name is Christine, but she goes by Christie. I'd say that's a good ice breaker, and a great story for her friends. 'Um, yeah, I met this cute chef. He works at a restaurant named after me.'" Liv smiles. "Why haven't you opened a restaurant named *Olivia's* yet? Don't you love me?" she jokes.

"That is just bloody fantastic. I would love to see Tex-Mex settle down with a lady."

"Well, we're doing our best, and it doesn't seem to be taking too much effort," she says as she heads back out front to check on things. A few minutes later, Tex-Mex moseys on back into the kitchen. I swear he had a little swagger going.

"How's it going out there?" I ask, trying not to probe for anything specific, hoping he'll offer up some dirt.

"I reckon they are lovin' this food," he says.

"Brilliant, that's great to hear. You deserve the credit; these were your menu items. Kudos," I say.

"Nah, teamwork," he says.

"What's that pretty lady that you were talking to eatin'?"" I inquire.

"I don't reckon she's tried anythin' yet."

"Then I guess you better whip something up real quick so ye keep her attention," I joke.

"What do you think I should make?" he asks.

"Anything you want, just make sure it includes love." I wink at him and he gives me a nod.

We are on our last wave and things are still on track. The reviews are fantastic, and I hear the girls starting the bidding for the auction. Multiple things are going for several thousand dollars.

It's getting close to midnight, and we've finished serving. I let the staff go out to mingle and watch the auction. We offer everyone champagne and have party favors and noisemakers, so they can be festive. I hear Jules start the countdown, "10-9-8-7-6-5-4-3-2-1 . . . HAPPY NEW YEAR!" she yells as "Auld Lang Syne" starts piping through the speakers. I grab Liv and pull her in for a kiss when she notices Tex planting a kiss on Christie's lips.

"I reckon Tex has got himself a girl," I claim.

CHAPTER FIFTEEN
(OLIVIA)

"We need to get busy," Garrett urges as we settle into the office at Gin & Tonic.

"I've put some things together on Pinterest. Think vision boards to spark ideas. We have an appointment at the Refinery in Los Angeles this Saturday to preview the space and put a deposit down for the engagement party. I think Valentine's Day will be perfect, but for the wedding . . ."

I interrupt, "I love all of your excitement and it all sounds fabulous, but I do have a couple non-negotiables. Hear me out before you respond. Tex-Mex has offered up his ranch in Dripping Springs, Texas to have the wedding." I see Garrett's expression turn to pure disgust.

"I know you're thinking it will be a muddy, stinky, hick venue, but I've seen pictures. The ranch is breathtaking. Fifty acres of lush landscape full of trees, ponds, and a river running straight through the property. It has *so* much potential. You can, of course, put your touch on it. We can make it a rustic glam wedding," I say, trying to get some level of excitement out of him.

Tristan chimes in, "Honey, it is *her* wedding. You have to let her create her own vision," then adds, "Liv, it sounds amazing. I'm sure whatever you choose will be fabulous." He gives Garrett that unspoken glare of *you better be nice* as he walks back upfront to tend to customers, leaving us to sort it out.

"Okay, give me some time to digest this. I had a whole different picture in my mind," Garrett relents, pacing back and forth.

"You can own the engagement party from start to finish. I will just show up. *I promise*. And, of course, I want your input on everything. This has nothing to do with me questioning your passion. I know you will only make it magnificent, but it is Finn's wedding, too. He needs to feel at home. Neither of us are fancy people. It needs to feel like us."

"I get it, *but* I am going to be involved every step of the way and need to have some veto power," he says.

"Deal," I agree.

"I made us an appointment at Stella's Boutique on Saturday morning in Beverly Hills to start shopping for wedding dresses. What month are we looking at?"

"Late September. That way it won't be too hot, plus Finn has his hands full with the food truck and the celebrity golf outing this summer. We want to go on a ten-day honeymoon."

"Where do you plan to go?"

"Finn is planning it. He mentioned Tulum, Mexico. It's in the Yucatan Peninsula. They call it the *Mexican Riviera*."

"Why don't you go to Hawaii or, better yet, Fiji or Tahiti?"

"We don't want to travel that far. We've heard great things about Tulum from Mac and Jules."

"Okay, well first things first. We have a full day planned on Saturday. Check out Pinterest. I started a wedding dress board too," he says with a big grin.

#

We drive down to Los Angeles late Friday evening. We are the first appointment at Stella's and have four consultants pulling gowns for us. Garrett has influence in this area with his semi-celebrity status. He's designed so many stars' homes that he's famous by proxy. It won't surprise me if he ends up with his own reality show someday, especially with connections like Mac and Finn.

I am set up in a giant dressing room. Garrett gets situated on the couch outside of my room in front of the floor to ceiling three-way mirror. Mimosas are flowing and the fashion show commences. They present me with twenty-five gowns to start. Sleek, satin, sequins, lace, tulle, sleeves, sleeveless, white and off-white. All of them are luxurious, but I'm looking for the perfect balance. Something that not only fits my body but is also appropriate for the venue. Nothing feels right, but Garrett forces me to try each to ensure I don't pass up on *the one*. Just as I'm about to give up, they come back with one more. It's an elegant, muted white, A-line dress. It has wide straps merged into a low neckline covered with a sheer overlay, giving it an overall modest but classic look. The back is half-opened. The fitted bodice is embellished with an embroidered applique. The skirt drapes and falls away perfectly from my body. As I step out of the dressing room, I hope Garrett's reaction reflects what I'm feeling inside because I *love* this dress. It's the only one that feels like me.

Garrett stands up in anticipation as I step out and onto the pedestal in front of the three-way mirror.

"What do you think?" I inquire.

"It's perfection. You look phenomenal. That's *the dress,*" he gushes.

"Promise? I was hoping I didn't have to sell you on it. I am *in love* with it."

"We'll take it," he says to the head consultant. "It's my treat, Liv."

"I haven't even checked the price. Are you sure?" I say as I check the tag then state, "Garrett, it's *thirty-eight hundred dollars.*"

"I don't want to hear another word about it. What are you thinking about a veil?" he asks, glossing over the cost.

"Something understated that clips into my hair, hanging down to my mid-back. For the reception, I'd wear a diamond embellished headband, no veil."

"Love it. Maybe you're better at this than I give you credit for." He smirks.

"I've learned from the very best." I lean in to give him a kiss on the cheek.

"Get dressed. We have to be over at the Refinery in thirty minutes for our tour and taste test."

#

The event planner greets us and escorts us up to the rooftop. The elevator opens to a lovely exquisite space with grand views of the city. The outer perimeter is framed by a twenty-foot wall, cut out into giant sections, mimicking floor to ceiling windows. Each individual area has private seating with a chandelier providing soft lighting. They are separated by large vases of voluminous flowers and greenery. There is an expansive swimming pool surrounded by a tiled deck.

"Thoughts?" Garrett says as I continue to take in the scenery.

"It's superb. Better than I could have imagined," I say, expressing my delight.

"We'd have this entire space all evening, so only our guests will be allowed entry. Of course, I will take care of all the details, but I want your approval on the setting."

"This is it," I respond.

"Great, let's do a taste testing to finalize the menu then leave the rest to me," he says as we are escorted back downstairs to the bar where they have a table set up.

It was a productive day. Finn drove down to meet me. Mac and Jules are having us overnight. Mac is on a three-month break from shooting his latest sitcom. The timing works out perfect with me being down here for the wedding appointments. Thankfully, everything has blown over and Jules never found out. *Thank God.* I can't believe how much a couple hours of drunkenness could impact my life. It's just a relief it's all out there and insignificant.

"Laddie, get in here, will ye," Mac says as he greets us with a hug, Julia in tow.

"Aye, I thought you were lettin' me cook for ye. It smells delicious," Finn remarks.

"Naw, it's yer night off. Yer our guest. Jules is making her famous lasagna," Mac says as they lead us to the kitchen for appetizers and cocktails.

"Finn, you seem like a lost puppy in this kitchen when you're not at the helm." Jules laughs.

"Aye, don't take it personal; I don't know how to sit in a kitchen. It's unnatural, but I'm grateful," Finn responds.

We polish off our second bottle of wine when Jules directs us to the dining room to sit down for dinner. She's prepared a large garden salad, lasagna, and homemade garlic bread. She learned a few things when traveling with Finn to the European festivals back in the day. Mac tops our glasses off with more red wine and proposes a toast.

"Tonight, we're celebratin' some *smashing* news," Mac says as he raises his glass. Finn and I glance over at each other, expecting the next words out of his mouth to be *Jules is pregnant*.

"I would like to congratulate the next famous screenplay writer . . . Olivia Henry." Finn and I look at each other, perplexed.

"Liv, remember when you were on set and I asked ye if I could pitch yer manuscript around?" Mac asks.

"Yes," she responds.

"*The Man Guide* received an offer from the Beyond Dreams Production Company for a hundred and twenty-five thousand dollars yesterday," Mac announces.

"*Bloody hell,*" Finn yells as he jumps up from his seat to kiss me. "This is brilliant. Absolutely brilliant." I sit, stunned, trying to process what was just said.

Tears stream down my cheeks as the shock settles in. "Are you kidding me? How? When?" I say in disbelief.

"My agent and I went to meet with the production company yesterday about another project and I pitched it. This story has legs, Liv. You have a natural talent."

"It's true. It's a gift," Finn chimes in. "You're making a connection between the beyond and those who are still here. Everyone has lost someone they love. People want to have faith that their loved ones aren't truly gone. You've told it in a funny and relatable way that they will embrace."

"He's right, Liv. I think this is going to explode," Mac says.

"Never in a million years could I dream this . . . I wrote this on a whim, as an escape to a place where Dan and I could exist in the same world. Imagining he's guiding me to my destiny from the other side. It's almost as if I'm manifesting it."

"I'm so proud of ye . . . and so is Dan," Finn gushes as his eyes well up with tears of pride.

"I really don't know what to say. How does this work? What happens next?" I inquire.

"We'll work out the details of the contract over the next few weeks. I recommend you use my lawyer to negotiate. He has a great deal of experience in this arena and I trust him with my life," Mac offers.

"That would be terrific. What about timing? I don't want this to interfere with the wedding planning."

"Welcome to Hollywood. There will be an eighteen month to two year waiting period for the studio to assign a director, producer, cast, crew, and allow them time to scout a location. There's lots to do."

"Well, that's comforting news. Will I get to be involved? What about with casting? I'd love to be on-set. I want to make sure it's portrayed with my vision."

"Of course. We'll write all those details into the contract. It's not uncommon for the screenplay writer to have heavy involvement in the creative process," Mac responds.

"Finn, pinch me. Is this really happening?" I say, overwhelmed with emotion.

"We are all thrilled for you, Liv. It couldn't be happening to a better person," Jules interrupts as she begins to dish out the lasagna. "Now, let's eat so we can get on to the celebrating."

Danny, I know you have everything to do with this. I'd be skeptical if I didn't know for certain that people will fall in love with our friendship and this eternal connection. In my darkest moments since you've passed—the terrorist attack, Owen being sick, and Finn walking away from me temporarily, I dove into writing this love story. The love letter to you about our friendship. It's the only thing that has gotten me through. I escaped into a world where you are guiding, directing, and comforting me. A place where I have nothing but faith. I realize now the path you're leading me down is the journey back to myself. You aren't going to give me my happy ending until I learn to love myself again and put all my trust into the bigger and better plan. I am getting in my own way with all my doubts and fears; I can see that clearly now. Thank you for your tremendous gift, for never giving up on me. I will love you forever and always.

Tonight is our engagement party. I've been so preoccupied with the screenplay negotiations it's a relief to know Garrett is on top of this. I know it will be magnificent. Finn and I are staying at the Bellaire Hotel in LA for the weekend, along with the rest of our out of town guests. Everyone flew in last night, and Jane, Red, Alexa, Liza, and I had a slumber party to pack in some quality girl time. Finn and I have such a busy schedule; I won't have time to fly back to Chicago this summer for a wedding shower, so the girls really want to spoil me this weekend. We are spending the day together getting manicures and pedicures before my friend Tracy comes to my hotel suite to do all our hair and makeup.

We arrive for our early morning appointments at the swanky hotel salon. The girls arrange for champagne, orange juice, fresh fruit, and pastries. We have a private area that has two large day beds surrounded with sheer, delicate curtains for us to lounge on while we wait to be called.

"Liv, can you believe it?" Jane asks. "Tonight is your *engagement* party. Remember how we dreamed about this day when we were little? We'd dress up in princess dresses and play house . . ." she says as her voice cracks.

"Aw, Jane are you getting choked up?" I lean over to grab her hand.

"I'm just so happy to see you so in love. We thought we lost you . . . when Dan died. You have your spark back. It's so wonderful to see," she says. "You're my best friend, and I just want to see you happy."

"Aww . . . don't make me cry," I whisper.

"We all feel the same way, Liv. We love you so much, and we *really* love Finn. He truly is your perfect complement. Your soulmate," Red adds.

"We all agree . . . " Alexa states and we all lean in to embrace.

"You are the best girlfriends anyone could ask for. How did I get so lucky?" I state.

"We want to give you something special before tonight," Red says, handing me a box.

"What's this?" I ask.

"Something we all put together for you." I unwrap the box to find a photo album wrapped in cream fabric, embroidered with the words *Beyond Love*. It's full of pictures from our night in Indianapolis—getting engaged and meeting Mellencamp.

I burst into tears. "Oh my gosh, this is so amazing," I gush. "I was so caught up in everything I didn't even notice all these moments," I say, clinging to the scrapbook. "One of the happiest nights of my life, and I'm so grateful each of you were there to share in it with me. What does the inscription mean?" I ask, flipping through the album.

"We thought it was the perfect phrase to capture the journey you and Finn have been on. Dan and Christine have been leading you together with their love from beyond. Poignant," Red says.

"I don't know what to say." I pause, getting choked up. "I will treasure this forever, thank you. . . "

Liza interrupts. "Okay, okay, enough with all the sap. What are you wearing tonight?" She breaks the emotional heaviness and we all start to laugh.

"Right, *priorities*. I'm wearing a high collar neck, knee length, navy blue satin dress with dangling, faux diamond earrings and three-inch, silver strappy sandals," I reply.

"Wow, it sounds *sexyyyy*," Liza says.

"You'll get a preview soon. You know Garrett. He had the perfect idea of what I should wear," I tease. "Thank God we have our very own stylist/decorator in the family. It takes off so much stress and pressure with shopping."

"What time does Finn get in?" Alexa inquires.

"He's helping Tex with prep then driving down from Palm Springs. We have strict orders from Garrett not to arrive a minute before seven thirty. He wants all the guests there by seven o'clock, so we can make an entrance. Of course," I say. "So be prompt."

Jules arrives to join us as Tracy is putting the final touches on my hair and makeup, and I take a deep breath to soak this all in. I'm full of nerves but in a good way. I want to take mental snapshots of everything happening to remember this moment forever. All the people I love will be in the same room to celebrate me, us. Finn is the perfect cherry on top of my life. *The happiest I've ever been.*

"Aye, ye all look smashing, especially this lassie," Finn says with a grin from ear to ear when I open the door to greet him. He grabs me and leans in for a kiss.

"Thanks, Finn. We're on our way over now to the Refinery now. We'll see you in about an hour or so," Red answers as she, Jane, and Jules leave the room, approaching the elevator.

"Stunning, Liv," he says as he grabs my hands to drink me in from head to toe. "I mean it. *Absolutely breathtaking* but pure torture. I want to rip that dress off ye this instant and take you right here."

"Well, then I probably shouldn't tell you I'm not wearing any underwear, should I?" I tease as he glides his hands across my ass, letting out a deep sigh and expressing his desire. "I promise to make it up to you the second we get home tonight. Now get in the shower or we'll be late."

Garrett has thought of every detail. We are welcomed by an entire wall of black and white photos of both Finn and I from childhood to present day and everything in between. Already speechless, I reach into my purse for a tissue as we turn to find a sea of our favorite faces awaiting our arrival.

Garrett approaches and inquires, "*Well*, how did I do?"

"Perfection. We are overjoyed. Thank you," I say, squeezing him tight.

"Honey, don't mess up that face. I have a photographer here. You can get mushy on me after eleven o'clock when everyone leaves. Let me show you around." He grabs my hand to tour the space. There must be ten thousand lights. Every tree is dripping in them, radiating and creating a romantic ambience. The pool is covered with floating flowers and candles. Two bars balance the space and a gourmet buffet lines the seating area on the far end of the pool. In the back corner is a sweets table with a multi-tiered, elegant cupcake tree. We spend the evening mingling with our guests. It's surreal to see everyone here celebrating us, to believe this is all really happening, and to know I have finally found a permanent home for my heart.

CHAPTER SIXTEEN
(FINN)

Jules arranges a surprise thirtieth birthday trip for Mac in Lake Tahoe. It's a quick, three-day ski weekend. He and I used to go to Switzerland to ski as kids, but that was a very long time ago. Liv hasn't ever skied. Since she grew up in the Midwest, she never understood why people who lived in a cold place would go to another cold place to vacation. She's much more of a beach girl. That said, she is excited to go and spend the weekend with them. Jules arranged for she and Liv to have a spa day while we spend a day on the black diamond slopes, so she is looking forward to getting pampered. Even with her lack of enthusiasm, I was able to convince her to sign up to take lessons for a couple days. Hopefully, I don't regret that decision.

After an eight-hour trek, we arrive before Jules and Mac. We're staying in a beautiful log cabin built into the edge of the mountainside for easy access to the slopes. The front is covered in windows with sprawling views of the lake. Mac tried to get me to meet him up here a couple times while I was working in Vegas, but I was always too busy. Now I see what I was missing. We get inside and unpack. We brought up a bunch of food, booze, and a birthday cake. Liv gets busy putting up some birthday decorations. Jules texts they are twenty minutes out. Mac thinks they're meeting Jules' family up here. I build a fire and put together a charcuterie platter so we have something to snack on.

"Aye, what are ye doing here?" Mac asks, entering the house.

"Surprising ye, ye bastart," I say, giving him a hug.

"This is *bloody fantastic*. I had no idea. Let's break out the whiskey and get this party started," he says.

"*Brilliant*,"

As we dive into the bottle, the girls pull out the spa brochure to pick out their various treatments. Outside of skiing, we plan to eat, drink, relax, and play games. Mac and Jules are really into trivia, plus we plan to play some euchre, Cards against Humanity, and whatever else we can find. Once the drinks are flowing, we decide to play a game of Pictionary. Girls against guys. It starts out civil then it gets more heated as the girls start to win. We are all very competitive.

"We used to play this back in high school," Liv says. "There were two teams. The word was 'coma.' Red was on my team. She starts creating an elaborate hospital bed, patient scenario, and I glance over at Dan's paper: he is drawing a half circle over and over. He thought the word was 'comma.' Hilarity ensued. Helps when you know how to spell."

We're down to the last round. The word is 'blinking.' It's my turn and I can't draw worth a damn, which is ironic since I'm right-brained. I start drawing an eye with eye lashes and an arrow pointing down.

Mac's shouting, "Eyeball . . . Eyelashes . . . Mascara . . . Winking . . ."

Then I hear Liv yell "Blinking" and they win the game. These girls are tough.

We break for dinner. I'm making mushroom risotto. They never expect me to cook because they want these get-togethers to be a vacation for me too, but it's what I love to do, especially for those I love the most. After dinner, we retire to the hot tub to take in the sky full of stars.

"So, Liv, I hear you're not much of a skier," Mac comments.

"I've actually only ever been once. We were home over Christmas break in college. Dan, Red, and some friends decided to go up to a ski resort in Wisconsin for New Year's Eve. Red was so hungover on the way up. She sat in the back of a Ford Explorer for almost four hours. She had her head buried in an empty Dorito bag she found under the seat, trying not to puke. She made it the whole way then got out to get some much-needed fresh air and Dan yells, 'Hey Red, *how about a greasy pork sandwich served in an ashtray?*' and she projectile vomited *everywhere*."

"Finn, the more I hear about this guy, I realize he would have been our third musketeer," he jokes.

"Oh, for sure," I add.

"So, did ye ski?" Mac asks.

"I paid two hundred dollars for ski clothing, another hundred on lodging, forty-five dollars in gas and tolls, followed by another hundred and seventy-five for all of the rental equipment and only made it down the hill once. On our first run, Red almost pulled a Sonny Bono. She had a total yard sale inches from a tree, and I tapped out. Not only was I scared out of my mind, but it was one of the most expensive days of my life," Liv states.

"*Bloody hell.* We'll make ye a skier before you leave here. Skiing out here is so different than the Midwest," Mac says.

"We'll see, but I wouldn't bet on it," Liv replies.

We turn in early because we have a big day of skiing ahead. Liv's anxiety alone will be enough to contend with.

#

It snowed several inches last night, so we'll have some nice powder today. We load the car with all our gear to find someone has etched a dick and balls into the snow covering our windshield.

"*Brilliant.* Looks like Dan visited us last night," I say to Liv, acting as if it's meant to be there.

"This is *one thousand* percent something Dan would have done to my car in the high school parking lot. Classic," Liv says, laughing.

We arrive at the main lodge and rent skis for Liv. She has a lesson starting at nine a.m. Her biggest anxiety is she thinks she's going to be in a class with all four-year-olds, so I spring and pay for a two-hour private lesson. I get her settled and right out of the gate can tell the instructor is a total pothead.

"Dude, what's up? I'm Nick." I look over at Liv who is rolling her eyes and mouthing, *Really?*

"Aye, man. Nice to meet ye. This my fiancée, Liv. She's a first timer. Think ye can help her?" I ask.

"Sure thing, dude. I'll have her on those runs by noon," he brags, pointing to the blue runs off in the distance. Liv is looking more frightened by the minute. It's not helping that Jules is a pretty decent skier, so she really is on her own.

"I'll be back to check on ye in a little bit," I say, leaning over to kiss her as she tugs on my coat, urging me to stay. "Ye'll be fine," I whisper.

I take off with Mac and Jules, and we ski some of the back runs for about an hour. I come back and find out Liv made it down the easiest green run without falling.

"Aye, ye did it," I congratulate her.

"Yeah, she did great, man. I think we should try another one," Nick says.

"I'm game. I'll come with ye. Whaddya say?" I say, trying to elicit some enthusiasm out of Liv.

"Okay, but I have to warn you; I have about another hour in me then I'm calling it," she says. I'm just happy she's trying it.

We get in line for the gondola, and I start making small talk with Nick to try to keep Liv distracted so she won't chicken out.

"So, Nick, how long ye lived here in Tahoe?" I ask.

"I grew up here. I started skiing real young so got a job here at the resort when I was fourteen so I could ski for free. I board, too," he says.

"Nice. Do you have a girlfriend?" I ask.

"Sometimes."

"What does that mean?" I ask, curious to hear the answer.

"Well, this place is so small. There are only like four chicks to every twenty dudes up here, so we just take turns. You date one for a while then you get back in line."

"Aye," I say, catching the *oh my God, he's got to be kidding* glare from Liv.

She makes it down like a champ without complaining, and we meet Mac and Jules in the lodge for lunch then call it an early afternoon. We have an early happy hour and a couple of rounds of games then eat dinner. Tonight, I went easy and made lasagna.

Everyone's beat. We're sitting around the fire, catching up.

"Jules, how is your brother doing?" Liv asks.

"He's declining every time I see him. Not major things, but I can see him really slowing down. He is so appreciative of everything we're doing. With the money we raised from the fundraiser at Christine's, they were able to build ramps to gain access to the house, they installed bars in all the bathrooms, and they installed a chair lift on their staircase. As the ALS progresses, he'll need more equipment. They plan to do some renovations on their first floor to turn it into a master suite, so he won't have to do the stairs."

"I hope these fundraisers help his local ALS Chapter and increase awareness so they can continue to get the support they need," Liv adds.

"My brother is really so grateful. My family can't thank you enough," Jules states.

"We wouldn't have it any other way," Liv declares.

"So, I have some news," I interject. "I haven't even told Liv this yet."

"You haven't? Well, then spill it. What is it?" she asks.

"You know how I surprised Liv at the Mellencamp concert to propose. . ." I begin.

"Yes," they respond.

"I actually flew in a day early, and I went to visit Mr. and Mrs. Francis." I pause as they all gasp. "It was the perfect opportunity. I had some things I wanted to give them from Paris. I wanted to tell them about Liv and how we met, and how I was planning to propose." I see Liv and Jules welling up with tears. "I told them about the connection between Dan and Christine. It ended up being such a cathartic visit. They were very sad to learn that Dan had passed. They remember him fondly. I told them about the signs and shared Dan's photo album from their European trip. Mrs. Francis took great comfort knowing they were together on the other side."

"Wow, that's so great, Finn. How thoughtful of you. I'm sure it meant the world to them," Liv says through her tears. "It makes me love you even more." She smiles.

"Truly, Finn. It's wonderful you did that for them," Jules adds.

"I had lunch with them and stayed for several hours. I wanted to go to the cemetery before it got dark; so as I was saying my goodbyes, Mrs. Francis handed me a letter Christine wrote to me before she passed. She said Christine made her promise to give it to me but insisted she wait long enough to ensure I had time to heal. So, here it is." I hold up the envelope.

"Oh my God, Finn, have you read it?" Liv asks.

"No, I waited. I wanted to be with all ye when I read it. I thought she might have a message for Jules and Mac in it, and it would give ye a chance to get to know her a little bit, too."

"Are you sure you want us here? Don't you want to read it in private?" Liv asks.

"You all watched me go through it. There's nothing she could say I wouldn't want ye to hear," I claim.

"If you're sure, we'd totally understand," Jules adds.

"I'm sure." I rip the envelope open to find two different notes, both short but labeled. I start to read aloud.

#1

My Dearest Finn,

I don't want you to be sad for me. I'm in a beautiful place; a place where there is no pain or suffering. A place where there is no time, only love in the truest form. I hope you've taken the time you need to grieve and given yourself space to heal, but what I want most is to know you are living a life of abundance. I hope you're reading this and your heart and soul are full and happy. My biggest wish for you is to find your next true soul mate. Someone beautiful who makes your heart soar, who makes you want to get out of bed every morning and live; someone who will love you without limits. Someone who sees your beautiful gifts and treasures every moment she gets to spend with you. Know that I did not ever want to leave you, but this is all part of God's plan. I will be watching over you and sending you signs to let you know I am right here with you always. God has big plans for you. He took me early because he needs me with him, but I know there are nothing but great things in store for you. Trust me.
I love you forever,
Christine.

I finish as both girls are wrapped around each other in tears, unable to speak.

"Should I read the other one?" I ask.

#2
Finn,
Okay, this one is a little lighter hearted. . .
First, please give my girl Jules the biggest hug imaginable and tell her how much I love and miss her. I will be watching over her too and will always be close. She's my best friend, won't ever leave her, and we're soul sisters."

I pause to do a temperature check on the room.

"Oh my God, I can't believe it," Jules says in amazement. "That may be the greatest gift anyone has ever given me . . . no offense, Mac . . . it's a girl thing," she says half laughing, half crying. "What does the rest say?"

"So, if you haven't found someone yet, do me a favor and look this girl up. Her name is Olivia Henry. You can probably find her on social media. She lives in Chicago. She's Dan's best friend from high school. He loved her as much as he loved me, more. Anyway, I never met her, but he never dated either one of us, which is miraculous. He always said she is spectacular, and spectacular is right up your alley. Plus, clearly, he has good taste in women he chooses to share his company with.
Nothing like getting dating advice from your dead wife, huh?
Love you,
Christine
XO.

Utterly speechless.

CHAPTER SEVENTEEN
(OLIVIA)

Garrett and I land in Austin to make the final arrangements for the wedding. We step out of baggage claim to meet our driver and the commentary begins.

"Honey, it's hot *as balls* out here. You sure you're sold on an outdoor wedding . . . where there are *farm animals?*" He is oozing sarcasm. "At least our town car will have air conditioning."

"You've never been to Austin. Give it a chance," I say, trying to calm his nerves.

"Not having a visual of this place is giving me anxiety," Garrett declares.

"You need to trust me. I've been watching the *best* for a long time. Maybe I do know what I'm doing," I joke.

It's about a forty-minute ride out to the ranch. It's beautiful, but Garrett has a point. We are *screwed* if it's this hot on September 29th. *Danny, please don't make me regret this decision.* We didn't pick the venue because Tex-Mex offered it or to save on costs. The thought of getting married outside, under the stars, seems romantic. Simple but elegant. That's why the wedding theme is rustic glam. Garrett can make *anything* fabulous.

"The city is not at all what I was expecting. I was envisioning cowboy boots and tumble weeds. There are some really cool areas around here," he admits.

"I'll take you into the city for dinner tonight. I'll bet you five-hundred bucks you'll fall in love with it before you leave. I seem to be right about these things," I say, confident.

We pull up and are greeted by a ranch hand, Jack, who is a friend of the family. Tex-Mex leases out the land to a local since he doesn't have any family left in the area. He's kept the property, thinking he'll return to his roots someday.

"Howdy, folks. I presume you're Olivia and Garrett," Jack says, extending his hand to shake Garrett's.

"Yes, thanks so much for meeting us," I reply. "We're so excited to see the property."

"Sure thing. Follow me," he says. We walk about an eighth of a mile to get to the barn. As we arrive, Garrett leans over and whispers to me.

"The first thing we're going to do is hire valets, so people don't have to walk 'cause *this* is bullshit." I turn to give him a glare.

"Y'all take as much time as you need. I've left this golf cart here for you to get around. Just mind your step. We do have scorpions and poisonous snakes round these parts," Jack says. Garrett turns and mouths *snakes*. "Here's my cell if you need anything. I'll leave you to it."

"Thank you so much," I reply, and we follow him outside to take in the scenery.

"Where to start," I say, scanning acre upon acre of lush land full of rolling hills, ponds, and trees that are hundreds of years old. "It's magical," I gush, mentally drifting off to visualize my perfect wedding day.

"How many extension cords do you think we'll need for all the portable air conditioning units? I'm literally sweating my ass off," Garrett quips, interrupting my fantasy.

"Give it a *chance*." I laugh. "I started a group text chat with the girls. I promised I would send them tons of pictures," I mention, snapping the view that looks out into the pasture from the barn. "And we need to FaceTime Finn . . . but let's walk around and get the lay of the land."

The barn is thirty-two feet tall with sixteen-foot walls and giant sliding doors. It's weathered; the paint is chipping, but it's been on the property since the seventies. The windows are dirty; several are cracked or broken, but we can spruce it up. It has charm. I am soaking it all in, envisioning the transformation Garrett will create. *Delicate elegance with an edgy vibe.*

We spend the next forty-five minutes walking the grounds. Garrett is busy sketching the space, taking notes. He directs me on occasion to take photos. I try not to interrupt him when he's in his zone. I distract myself by texting a dozen pictures to the girls.

OLIVIA: Soooo, what do you think?

RED: *Wow. Liv, it's amazing!*

JANE: *Perfection!*

ALEXA: *Stunning!*

LIZA: *Beautiful!*

OLIVIA: Yeah, I'm so glad you guys love it. It's even more mesmerizing in person.

RED: So happy for you.

JANE: Wish we were there.

ALEXA: Enjoy every minute.

LIZA: Have fun.

OLIVIA: Okay, Garrett is ready to give us a rundown of the plan. Love you guys! XO.

I text the pictures to Finn a few minutes before we FaceTime him, so he can get a feel for the property.

"Hey Finn, "Garrett says as Finn's handsome face pops up on the screen.

"Laddie, thanks so much for doing this for us. I know this is your specialty but am still sorry I couldn't get away to join ye," Finn replies.

"Finn, the property is *magnificent*. The pictures don't nearly do it justice." I gush with exuberance. "It's going to be spectacular. I can't wait to hear Garrett's vision. He will transform this place into a fairytale, won't you?"

"I will say I kept my expectations low, but yes, we can definitely work with this," Garrett replies.

"Buckle up. Here goes. As guests arrive, they'll be greeted by wooden signs, made from old shipping palettes, with arrows pointing to the different sections, directing them to the ceremony, cocktails, fire pit, dancing . . ." He's pointing to each area in his notebook to give Finn an idea of how the grounds are laid out. "The ceremony will be set up over here in this area. Plush, hundred-year-old oak trees surround an enclosed, intimate space. It will provide the perfect amount of shade. We'll set up ten rows of long bench seating and old wooden tree stumps, facing the large pond. The ceremony will be at dusk, so, there will be a sparkle to the water." He pauses. "We good so far?"

"Aye. It's *brilliant*, please continue," Finn assures.

"A white runner for you to walk down the aisle and a wicker arch in front of this pier for you to exchange vows, surrounded with flowers and greenery," Garrett adds.

"Finn, it's hard to describe, but it really *is breathtaking*," I declare.

"Aye. I believe ye. Tex-Mex wouldn't steer us wrong," Finn responds.

"Next up, the cocktail hour will be set up over here," he says, circling his notebook. "It's a flat area covered in dirt about ten yards from the barn."

I interrupt "There's lots of dirt, so we better *pray* it doesn't rain."

"I'll arrange that with Tex-Mex as well," Finn jokes.

"Imagine old wine barrels holding large charcuterie boards full of meat, cheese, and other hors d'oeuvres. We'll get dozens of wine bottles produced with custom labels with your initials and wedding date. I'll have lanterns strung from these tree branches," he says, walking toward the trees to give Finn a visual. He points to the waist-high, prairie split fence adding character. "A large fire pit over here, staged with big baskets of white, fluffy throws embroidered with the words '*McDaniels Wedding*' for guests to take home, surrounded by white Adirondack chairs, a s'more's bar, and tubs full of sparklers." He rattles off details as he leads us back inside the barn.

"Obviously, all this machinery will be removed to create one large, open space. I'll break it up into quadrants to make it feel like multiple rooms. For dining, envision three long, handmade aged oak tables stretching across the floor to both ends." I turn my phone so Finn can get perspective.

"I don't know if you can see the floors Finn, but they are aged, wide planked tobacco pine wood floors. Very rustic," I add. "And look at these hammer beam trusses on the ceiling."

Garrett continues, "Community dining for thirty at each table covered with formal table cloths. The chairs will be causal but comfortable, spray painted in silver. Wild flowers in mason jars will serve as centerpieces in front of every other place setting, along with dozens of lit candles. We'll set up the gourmet buffet in the northeast corner and have bars at both the north and south ends of the barn with a dance floor in the southeast corner." He pauses.

"Still with us?" I ask, making sure he's still on board and doesn't feel like our wedding is being hijacked.

"*Aye*." He nods.

"I'll weave soft, white linen fabric throughout the rafters and hang six giant crystal chandeliers from bulky chain link in the ceiling. In between, we'll have light bulb lights dangling from exposed electric cords over the tables. These support beams will be wrapped from ground to ceiling with white lights, creating ambience. I'll also have trees and potted plants placed throughout the space, bringing the outdoors in. I'll cover these walls with faux curtains. We'll have an over-the-top dessert bar line the back section over here. About an hour before the reception ends, we'll set up a gourmet burger bar for people to soak up all the alcohol. The last fifteen minutes I'll lead everyone outside to light candles in flying paper lanterns, make wishes, and then release them into the sky as we send you off." He finally takes a breath and looks at me for my reaction.

"You are nothing short of *amazing*," I say with a tear running down my cheek. "I couldn't dream of anything more perfect."

"I'm speechless lad, absolutely glorious," Finn adds.

"Don't get sappy on me yet. We've got a ton more to do, but *I guess* I can make this work." He bursts into laughter.

"I am confident ye can handle it. I have to get back to the kitchen so will drop off, but Liv, it's absolutely smashing. I can't wait to be your husband."

"Aww, me too," I gush.

"Send me photos of the rest of it. I love you," he says.

"I love you, too."

Garrett and I take the golf cart out to the old stables to feel out the space for the rehearsal dinner, which will be more laid back and casual. We're having a pig roast. Tex-Mex is cooking.

"We don't want to duplicate the wedding, so we'll mix it up. We'll have casual picnic tables with overflowing vases of sunflowers lining the table. The buffet will be set up over here. We'll serve the food out of bushel baskets. I'll individually wrap the silverware in recyclable brown paper bags decorated with pig stamps. The general seating areas will consist of bales of hay and tree stumps. I'll put a bourbon shot bar with custom shot glasses. We'll have barrels of wine tapped, and wheel barrels stuffed with iced cold beer. We'll use the stables for outdoor games like bocce ball, croquet, horseshoes, giant Jenga, and corn hole with personalized black and white, bride and groom, boards. I'll throw in a few more of my touches to glam it up for a bit, but you get the picture," he says.

"Even though we're having all the weekend festivities here at the ranch, I want the two nights to feel distinctly different."

"Your plan sounds terrific," I respond.

"Our driver is here to pick us up, so we need to head back," Garrett informs. "Next up, lodging."

Tex-Mex suggested we have our guests stay in Fredericksburg. It's a sleepy little German village in the heart of Texas hill country. It's known for its small-town charm offering antiquing, galleries, boutiques, and wineries. Garrett approves after he tours and meets the owners of The Hayden Run Falls Inn. We have reserved the entire inn to house our eighty-five guests from Thursday to Sunday. The size of the property is perfect. They have a main building with sixty guest rooms, along with two dozen small cabins and cottages spread across the sprawling countryside near the picturesque Hayden Run Falls. It has a bed and breakfast feel to it and offers shuttles into town for guests extending their stay. We'll arrange for trolleys to transport guests back and forth to the ranch for the designated wedding festivities.

Danny, what do you think? Isn't it fabulous? Is this not going to be the best wedding a girl could ask for? The only thing that would make it perfect is having you there. Thank you from the bottom of my heart for helping me find Finn. I am so grateful. I'm finally overwhelmed with joy and happiness rather than darkness and despair. I will never accept that you won't be here with me, but I know you will be here in spirit and I love you. Forever.

We get back into the town car and head into the city of Austin to check into our hotel for the night. We take a nap, shower, and arrive at Abel's on Lake Austin before sunset to discuss details from the jam-packed day. The sprawling water views are the perfect backdrop.

We are seated at our table on the deck, order cocktails, and get down to business.

"I must admit; I had a horrible picture of this place in my mind. Tex-Mex showed me some photos, but they weren't overwhelming. I couldn't get a vibe, but I think Austin might become one of my favorite cities. It's incredibly charming. Nothing like what I expected. I guess that's the snobby Californian in me. "I won't go as far as fawning apologies, but here is your five hundred dollars." He passes me five one-hundred-dollar bills across the table.

"I hate to say I told you so, but *I told ya, I told ya,*" I sing. "I had no doubt you would fall in love with this place. It has a special way of capturing your heart." I gesture to the view. We pause when the waitress returns with our cocktails to look over the menu and order, so we aren't interrupted.

"Now, let's talk specifics," he begins. "Who are you having stand up in the wedding?"

"Jane will be my matron of honor. Red will be the only bridesmaid, and, of course, Livey and Owen will be the flower girl and ring bearer. They will walk Frank, Finn's pup, up the aisle,"

"Aw, so cute. Who will Finn have?" he asks.

"Mac will be his best man, and he wants *you* to be his only groomsman," I say.

"*Really*? I'm so touched."

"What are you thinking about colors? Flowers? Dresses?" he inquires.

"For dresses, I was thinking about dark charcoal. It's classic but delicate. Flowers are where we can infuse all the color. I was thinking fuchsias, lavender, and deep purples with white interspersed," I add as the waitress delivers our food. The patio is packed. Not an empty table in sight. Austin is another city where you have outdoor living almost year-round. So many quaint towns and neighborhoods with great food and live music. If I get tired of the desert, this would be next on my list. So grateful to Tex-Mex for his gift.

"I'm *very* impressed. You are dialed in on the details," he comments. "I received several highly recommended local vendors from my clients that are familiar with the area. A flower shop called Tiny Bouquets. They specialize in wild flowers grown seasonally in this local market. I think they would be perfect to hire as the florist. For the catering, Tex-Mex recommended a place called Forks & Spoons that does high-end catering. Things like grilled veal, filet. I feel like since we're having this on a ranch, people will be expecting a menu heavy with meat. We can add a fish option like crab stuffed shrimp, ahi tuna, or red snapper. We'll keep the rehearsal focused on pork and chicken BBQ."

"Sounds perfect," I reply. I know I should be throwing a tantrum about some of these decisions at some point, but the truth is I couldn't feel more relaxed relinquishing all the details to Garrett. He would never disappoint me.

"For sweets at the rehearsal, I was thinking of a cupcake tree surrounded by large bowls of sweet candies like Sour Patch Kids, Jelly Bellies, gummy bears, Sprees, Lemon Heads, and Red Hots. I think that would be festive and go along with the games. For the wedding, we'll have an extravagant chocolate sweet table with individual tiramisu jars, chocolate covered strawberries, pretzels, Oreos, and fruit with a chocolate fondue fountain. The wedding cake will be a multi-tiered, lemon layer cake," he suggests.

"I love all of it," I say, agreeing.

"What about music?" he inquires.

"I plan to hire a bag piper to surprise Finn right after we exchange our vows, so don't let the cat out of the bag. It's my way of bringing some of his Scottish heritage into the ceremony," I say.

"He will *love* that," Garrett gushes. "That is really sweet."

"Thanks. I don't get many opportunities to do nice things for him, so I think this will really touch him," I say. "Now as far as the music for the overall reception, I'm torn. I can either go with a country band that can sing some classic rock songs or go with the standard DJ. I'm not going to lie; my friends love to dance and can get doooown. I think they would choose the DJ," I convey as we pause to take in the beautiful sunset. I am falling more in love by the minute. This place is breathtaking.

"I have the perfect idea. Let's hire the band to sing at the rehearsal dinner, and we'll have the DJ play at the wedding reception?"

"Problem solved. Excellent idea," I respond.

"I'll take care of calling and reserving everything. I know you're splitting everything with your parents so will negotiate the best rates I can. I have special powers and can offer some non-tangible perks," he states. "So, I guess that leaves only one thing."

"What's that?" I question.

"You are responsible for mother nature delivering perfect seventy-five-degree weather with blue skies and sunshine for the ceremony and cocktail hour. Then it can dip into the mid-sixties after sunset for the reception. Think you can make that happen?" he jokes.

"I'll get Dan all over it," I respond.

CHAPTER EIGHTEEN
(FINN)

We arrive in the Hamptons for the ALS fundraiser for Kevin. Sadly, he can't travel to be a part of it because he isn't feeling up to it, but we are bound and determined to raise as much money as possible. Based on the size of the security building in the gated community we're approaching, that shouldn't be a problem. We have to show ID to be cleared for entry. I've never seen anything like it. We're approved and given directions to the house that consists of "take a left at that mansion, then turn right before you hit the Queen's house." We pull up to a ten-thousand square foot, grand Cape Cod home. It's practically a *palace*. Garrett emerges from the front door in the only dramatic way he knows how to welcome us. Tristan mentioned this cost him a mere forty-five thousand dollars to rent for the week. Maybe we should have had him just write a check and saved everyone the trouble.

It's a twelve-bedroom, sprawling estate on the dunes of East Hampton. He takes us on a tour of the house that will require a map to navigate. We walk the lush grounds and end at our room for the next four nights. We're staying in the pool house, casita, or McMansion; whatever you prefer to call it. I just know that it's nicer than my *entire* house. It has two floors, a chef-grade kitchen, and its own pool. I know—the *irony*.

Today is the last day of the celebrity golf outing, so we're having the fundraiser tomorrow night. We'll get two extra nights to relax on the back end, but until then, this trip is all business. Tex-Mex is flying in later today and meeting me over at the polo grounds for our final walk-through. We have two hundred guests coming. Everyone from celebrities to New York financiers and socialites.

Liv is focused on the silent auction items.

"Okay, so what do we have?" Liv asks Garrett.

"We have eight four-by-four paintings from an up and coming artist in SoHo. I bought two of his pieces for one of my clients and fell in love with his work. It's high-end abstract art. He has a unique technique. He'll be on-site, working on a painting, so guests can talk to him about his process. So envision a mini-gallery. Those alone should sell for ten to twelve thousand easily. Maybe we can get people into a bidding war," Garrett quips. "We are also auctioning off Finn for a night. That could be anything from a small intimate dinner to a large gathering. We'll just have to see and drive the price up. We have some international golf packages, a glam safari to Africa, a wine making experience at a vineyard in Napa, and a VIP tour of the Bourbon Trail."

"Wow, those all sound incredible. Be honest; what is the number you have in your head that you're expecting to raise?" I ask.

"I think between the silent auction and other donations, we can easily make two hundred and fifty thousand," he replies.

"That would be terrific. Let's hope you're right. You're usually spot on about these things," I say.

"Finn, how are you feeling?" Garrett asks.

"Aye, brilliant. Tex-Mex should be landing in a few hours then we'll regroup and finalize everything for tomorrow," I reply.

"Where did we land on the menu?" he inquires.

"It will be a little bit of everything. We plan to have a few of our new menu items from our event in Palm Springs: charcuterie platters, fig and olive tapenade, ahi tuna bites, crab stuffed mushrooms, and lobster croquettes. We wanted to go somewhat heavy on the seafood, given the venue," I reply.

"Sounds scrumptious," Garrett answers as Tristan appears with drinks for us.

"Did he tell you the story yet?" Tristan asks with a smirk.

"What story?" I ask.

"About the forty-five hundred dollars he spent on the free painting he was given?" Tristan continues.

"Ohhhh . . . this should be good," Liv comments. "Do tell."

"So, we meet with this artist for lunch back in LA. He was interested in gifting Garrett a painting, so he would consider recommending him or using him for projects in the future. Let's be honest; Garrett saw a piece he wanted but didn't want to pay for it so pitched the guy about how he has all these high-end clients that come through his home and would see his incredible work. You know, laying it on thick. So, he convinces this guy to give him a particular piece. Again, for free," Tristan mentions.

"We're with you so far," Liv states.

"Well, the painting is big. It's at least four by four, but we manage to squeeze it in the car," he continues. "That's when all the fun starts. The artist is now long gone. We're still out shopping and Garrett sees this kitchen island that he just *has to have* and asks the store if they can *hold* his painting for him until he can come back to retrieve it. They reluctantly agree. So fast forward a couple days, Garrett's car goes into the shop for a few days, and the store owner is now calling and demanding he come and get the painting, which, as a reminder, is not *their merchandise.*"

"Oh my God, I don't know where this is going, but this is already hilarious. To recap, this is the *free* painting that he finagled then abandoned for the next shiny object less than an hour later . . . okay, got it. I'm all caught up. Please continue," Liv says.

"So, Garrett pushes the problem off on to me and tells me to go pick it up. I try three different cars; none of them are big enough to fit the painting. On the fourth trip, five days later, the store owner suggests we remove the canvas from the frame in order to get the painting in the car and take it to a professional to have it reframed. *Genius*. Now, the artist keeps texting Garrett to send him a photo of the painting hanging in his home, so he can use it for his portfolio, which of course we do not have because it is now being reframed," he says.

"Sorry to interrupt," Liv says as she looks over at Garrett. "You know you are pathetic, but this is why we love you."

"So fast forward even further, we need to rent a truck to retrieve the newly framed painting and Garrett rear ended someone in the parking lot when he picked it up . . . " he says and Liv interjects. "Costing him forty-five hundred dollars," and the hilarity ensues.

"Ye can't make this shit up," I add.

"How he convinced an artist to bring eight paintings to giveaway at this event tomorrow is *beyond* me," Tristan finishes.

We go back to our room to unpack and settle in.

"We seem to be going from one thing to another these days," I say to Liv.

"I know. Can we officially start the countdown to our wedding? I want nothing more than to kiss your sexy, naked body all day for ten days straight," she responds with a flirty grin.

"Well, my dear. I think we should practice. How about we spend the next hour pretending we're on our honeymoon?" I say, reaching for her hand and leading her into the bedroom.

It's a gorgeous, eighty-five-degree day with a light breeze off the water. Perfect day for a fundraiser.

The girls are dressed to the nines. Liv is wearing a smashing spaghetti strap, fuchsia lace dress that hits her just above her knees. She has her hair pulled back off her face and looks absolutely radiant. It's these moments where I pause to look at her and wonder how I got so lucky. Here she is, in the Hamptons, hosting a fundraiser for my best friends whom she met less than a year ago. She is so gracious, thoughtful, and giving. She's done nothing but throw herself into these events as if Kevin were her own brother, utter selflessness.

Guests start arriving and mingling. I'm thinking I saw Tiger Woods and Martha Stewart. How is *that* for an attendee list? Cocktails are flowing and pocketbooks are starting to open. Jules and Mac are making their rounds to see how we are faring. They notice there's a bidding war going on with my item. The *hire a chef for a day*. It's already over one hundred thousand dollars. I mean, I'm humbled, but I'm not the pope. Jules, who is emceeing the event, gets on the mic and lets the guests know we will be closing the silent auction in thirty minutes and to go cast their final bids.

Winners are announced one by one from lowest to highest. I keep waiting to hear my item called. I hear all the paintings sell, then the Bourbon Trail, wine experience, and golf trip followed by the safari. The last item is mine. So far, they have raised one hundred and sixty thousand dollars.

"And the final auction item of the evening, "Jules starts, "is the chef for a day featuring our very own Finn McDaniels, owner and head chef of Christine's in Palm Springs," she says as the crowd applauds. "And the winner is Caroline Hargrove, who purchased Finn to cook for her wedding reception in New York City for two hundred and fifty thousand dollars, bringing our grand total for the night to four hundred and ten thousand dollars." *Holy shit, who is this chick and why does she want a quarter of a million-dollar meal at her wedding reception?*

Jules continues, "On behalf of everyone from the ALS Foundation, we'd like to thank each and every one of you for your extreme generosity to this very important cause so close to my heart."

Liv approaches. "I had no idea what your worth is, daaaaarrrrrllllling?" she teases.

"Who is that woman?" I ask.

"She's some hoity-toity, high-brow, snobby socialite," she reveals.

"Ohhh, do I detect a little jealousy around your quarter-million-dollar fiancé?" I joke.

"Let's just hurry up and get back to our pool house so I can show you that *I'm* priceless."

CHAPTER NINETEEN
(OLIVIA)

"Good morning, beautiful," Finn whispers, kissing my neck. Frank is laying on the floor beside the bed.

"Mmmm. You can keep that up, mister," I respond.

"Do you know what today is?" he asks.

"What?" I inquire.

"It's the last day we'll be in this bed before we become husband and wife," he gushes, rubbing my back.

"I know. As excited as I am to get to Austin to start all the wedding festivities, I don't want to leave your side. I miss you already," I say.

"Well, I think we need to make our last day being single special so we always remember it."

"What did you have in mind?" I ask while stroking his ass.

"I think we start the day by making love in every room of this house. Then I'll make you breakfast. We take Frank for a hike, soak in the hot tub with champagne, then you host a bachelor party for one and strip for me tonight after I make you dinner. What do you say?" he suggests, kissing my body from head to toe.

"I'd say that we have a busy day, so we should get started," I quip, pulling him in for a passionate kiss.

I don't know how it's possible, but I love him more *every single day*. It's getting harder and harder to be away from him, even when he's at the restaurant. We've already been through a lifetime together with everything that's happened. I look forward to being a boring married couple.

OLIVIA: *Well girls, I just finished packing for MY WEDDING.*

RED: *Yay! It's finally here. Soak up every beautiful moment.*

JANE: *I can't wait to see you! Livey and Owen can't wait to see you.*

ALEXA: *We can't wait to get there.*

LIZA: *Yeah! Happy Wedding Week!*

#

OLIVIA: *We landed safe.*

FINN: *I miss you so much already.*

OLIVIA: *Me too. Pure torture. Hurry up and get here. I love you so much.*

FINN: *I love you more. Kisses.*

Garrett and I arrive in Austin early Wednesday morning to put all the last-minute details in place. We meet Red, Jane, Alexa, and Liza at the airport. We all scheduled flight arrivals at the same time. We'll take today to settle in then we have an early morning manicure, pedicure, and massage appointments for a final day of pampering. Everyone else is flying in tomorrow night, including Finn and his parents. The best news is the forecast looks amazing. It's seasonably cool for this time of year, so it will be between the high seventies to low eighties during the day and high sixties in the evening.

Danny, this is it. It's finally here. I'm getting married. I'm so ready to marry this man. My heart is full. You know what I want from you for as a wedding present? Two things: 1. Can you please pull some major strings upstairs with mother nature to keep it sunny and cool for the next five days? 2. Send me something on our wedding day so I know you're there with us. Of course, I know you will be, but I want something big to feel your presence. Surprise me.

Garrett and I send the girls to the inn to check-in, and we go straight to Tex-Mex's ranch. We arrive at the same time as the event company dropping off all the tables, chairs, and equipment. Set up will begin in the morning, along with the final walk-through of the property with the caterer, florist, and musicians. Next, we go to Hayden Run Falls Inn. We deliver the welcome packages for the guests, which is a goodie bag full of brochures of things to do in the area, a thank you note from Finn and I for joining us on our beautiful day, and a custom picture frame to place a photo in from this weekend. The inn owners take us to tour the honeymoon suite. It's the farthest cabin on the property. The porch is in direct line of sight to the Hayden Run Falls. It's spectacular. Lastly, we meet up with the girls in the lobby and go to the boutique to pick up my dress for the rehearsal dinner.

"Go try it on," Garrett demands as he pulls me toward the dressing room. It's a crisp, white, long-sleeved, above the knee, crocheted Michael Kors dress.

The girls crowd around. "Well, what do you think?" I ask, spinning around for the reveal.

"You look stunning, Liv," Red gushes as all the girls fawn over me.

"I'm thinking you won't be eating any BBQ pig," Garrett quips. "How did this menu get past me? What was I thinking?"

I laugh. "I'll only eat white things, like popcorn. . . " I joke when he interrupts.

"And air."

Tonight is the rehearsal dinner. Finn and I agreed to stay in separate rooms before the wedding tomorrow. He is waiting in the lobby with Tristan. Tracy is putting the final touches on my hair and makeup when Garrett knocks on the door.

"We're ready to go over to the ranch for the rehearsal," he states.

"Okay, let's go. Tracy, we'll see you over there. My friends Liza and Alexa will meet you in the lobby in thirty minutes to ride with you," I say as we walk over to meet the guys. As soon as we turn the corner into the lobby, I lock eyes with Finn. My heart sinks and the butterflies take over. I run the last few steps to embrace him.

"Aye, I'm speechless. Truly. There isn't a word perfect enough to capture your beauty," he says as he leans in to kiss me.

"You look pretty sexy yourself, Mr. McDaniels," I flirt, grabbing his hand as we follow Garrett and Tristan to the car.

Everything looks amazing. Garrett did such a great job with his vision. It's casual but not at all cheesy. He manages to keep it high end so people don't feel like they're standing in dirt. Guests are starting to arrive, everyone is settling in, and cocktails are flowing. Mac and Finn's dad, Alistair, start the crowd on the bourbon shots. Great ice breaker. My mom and Finn's mom, Fiona, are tucked away in a corner, chatting up a storm. Finn and I took both sets of parents to dinner in Fredericksburg last night to get them introduced. They hit it off and seem like lifelong friends, which warms both of our hearts.

Tex-Mex announces dinner is ready, so everyone starts making their way through the buffet line. A little while later Mac approaches the stage to take the mic from the band.

"Good 'evenin," Mac starts. "Thank ye for coming . . . I'd like to propose a toast. I've known Finn since the day we were born. His mum and da were my second mum and da. We grew up like brothers. We've been through a lot together over the years. Some happy, some tragic, but we always come out better blokes in the end. I couldn't think of anyone more perfect for Finn than Olivia. She has captured his heart in a way I've never seen. They are true soulmates and have two guardian angels to prove it. So, please, raise yer glasses with me to wish 'em well. There is an old Scottish proverb that says, 'friendship stands not in one side.' Cheers, lads," he finishes, gesturing over to us when I see Red making her way to the stage. My heart is in my throat and I well up with tears. Red is my rock. My oldest and dearest friend. She was with me in the emergency room when we got the news that Dan didn't make it. Life as I knew it stopped that day for a long time. She put aside her own sadness to take care of me. I wouldn't have survived without her. I am eternally grateful for her unconditional love and support.

"Hi everyone, I'm Red. Liv's best friend," she begins. "I'd like to mirror what Mac just said. I've known Liv most of my life. I've been waiting for this day for a long time. I've seen Liv at her worst, and I can say without hesitation that she is now at her absolute best. Finn, you are the perfect complement to my best friend. You make her happier than I even thought was possible. So, welcome to the family. We love you and know you will take exceptional care of our girl. I will leave you with this Corinthians passage . . . 'now these three remain: faith, hope, and love. But the greatest of these is love.' Cheers, everyone." Red finishes, handing the mic back to the band then walks over to embrace Finn and me.

"Red, I love you so much," I gush as tears stream down my face.

"I love you too, Liv. Today is the beginning of the best chapter," she whispers in my ear.

Finn and I make our way up to present our bridesmaids and groomsmen with their gifts.

"First, I'd like to start by thanking ye for being here with Liv and I as we start our life together. We couldn't be happier. All of you mean the world to us, so it means everything that yer here. I'd especially like to thank Mac, my brotha from anotha mutha," he says in his best hillbilly rap accent, eliciting laughter. "I truly don't know what I'd do without ye. And to Garrett, who was one of the very first people I met in

Palm Springs. Ye not only helped me with my restaurant, but yer the reason I'm standin' here today. I met Liv because of ye, whether you wanted me to or not," he says. "Here is a small token of my appreciation for standing by me through thick and thin." He hands them small boxes that hold personalized silver flasks. "This should help with the bourbon consumption."

Finn hands me the mic. I suddenly feel light-headed and my palms start sweating. I'm so overcome with emotion looking at this room full of people. I realize the impact they've all had on my life. I realize I am never the center of attention, so I'm a bit overwhelmed. I take a deep breath to calm down. *Danny, help me get through this.*

"I only have one blood sister whom I adore more than anyone or anything in the world, but life has blessed me with a spectacular sisterhood of women. We don't share a bloodline, but they are my family. These women have, most literally, carried me through the worst days of my life. It is my biggest honor to have them by my side as I enter the happiest moment in my life. Even when I lost all faith, hope, and love you let me, without hesitation and with full hearts, borrow yours. For that, I am eternally indebted to each of you. There is no gift profound enough to express my gratitude," I declare. "This goes beyond just Jane and Red. I want to also share this moment with Lisa, Alexa, Tracy, and Jules. You are all amazing women that have done nothing but enrich my life, and for that, I will love you forever. This is just something small to serve as a reminder to always believe." As they all approach, I hand them each a box that contains a bangle bracelet with a believe charm and their initials.

"Now, let's dance," the lead singer shouts and begins playing "What I Like About You" by The Romantics. I grab Finn's hand, and we go out to the dance floor with everyone and bust a move until we are soaked in sweat. The band finally slows it down to give people a breather and they start singing Madonna's "Crazy for You".

Finn interrupts, "Excuse me lassies, but I would like to slow dance with my future wife," he says, spinning me around. He wraps his arms around my waist and pulls me in close, placing his forehead to mine. Suddenly, the crowded dance floor goes quiet and all I can see is him.

"Hi. We're getting married tomorrow," I whisper in his ear.

"Aye. I can't wait. How did I get so lucky?" he asks.

"No, I'm the lucky one. I never want to spend another day without you," I say just before I kiss him.

"Me either. I don't know how I'm going to make it to tomorrow morning without ye in my arms," he says. "Wanna go down to the pier and make out one last time?"

"I thought you'd never ask," I declare.

The girls arrive to the room early with coffee in hand, ready to get primped for the big day ahead. My mom, Fiona, and Livey will be here in a couple hours for their session. Tracy wastes no time since she has eight of us to tend to. The photographer will be here at noon for pictures of the wedding party. Finn and I won't do any combined photos until after the ceremony. I want the first time he sees me to be when I walk down the aisle.

All the guests are seated when we arrive. We duck into the barn for privacy until the ceremony begins, when my dad comes back to see me for the first time.

"Sweetheart, you look beautiful," he says with a tear in his eye. "I know you doubted this day, but I always knew you'd find him. Finn is a good, good man. He'll take care of you. I'll always be the first and last man to ever love you, but I'll let him borrow you for these middle years."

"Thanks Dad, I love you," I say, welling up with tears. "It took a while to find him because he has giant shoes to fill," I finish, leaning over to give him a kiss.

"I love you, too," he says as the music starts playing.

"That's our cue," Red says as she starts up the aisle, followed by Jane, then the twins pulling Frank in a wagon.

"Time to roll," my dad says, smiling before kissing me on the cheek when we hear the violinist start playing the wedding march. We begin our short trek. I see Finn and tears fill my eyes, knowing I've been waiting for this moment my whole life. As I get closer, I see he's wearing Chuck Taylors. I gasp and have to catch my breath.

"You okay sweetie?" my dad asks, sensing my sudden change in demeanor from the shock.

"Everything is perfect," I respond and continue up the aisle.

Danny, you absolutely overwhelm me. Thank you.

We arrive and my dad hugs me then turns to Finn and whispers, "Take good care of my baby."

"Aye, Mr. Henry, only the very best," he responds then turns to me and whispers, "Liv, you look *ravishing.*"

"I hope you're not wearing anything under that kilt," I joke, then move in closer to and lift up my dress just enough to reveal my Chuck Taylor tennis shoes.

"These are my something old," I say.

"I wanted to surprise ye," he responds. We both chuckle through our tears, lock hands, and then face the priest.

We finish our vows, and the priest introduces us to the crowd when the bagpiper begins to play. Everyone turns to watch the Scotsman approach. I have my eyes glued to Finn. He is in awe. *Stunned.*

"Liv, yer amazing. Thank you," he says, kissing me.

"I wanted to surprise you," I say, rubbing his back as he takes in the moment.

The reception is underway. It's the first chance I've had to take everything in. The venue is nothing short of magical. Garett's vision is in full force. Any girl would kill for this atmosphere. The best part about it is it looks effortless. *Magnificent.*

Once everyone is seated, my dad stands up to say a prayer and bless our food.

He continues, "Thank you everyone for coming this evening and joining our families on this very joyous occasion. As parents, one of the hardest things in the world is to witness a child's heartbreak. As many of you know, Liv lost her best friend Daniel several years ago, and we thought we'd lost her dazzling personality. He was such a unique and special young man. He radiated sunshine wherever he went. Our family loved him as one of our own, and we all miss him dearly. I know Finn has been through a great tragedy as well with the loss of his first wife, Christine. These are very long and tough roads for such young lives to navigate. Pain I never faced and wounds I would never be able to mend. Hard for a parent to come to terms with. What I will say is that my faith grew stronger as I witnessed these two souls being brought together by their loved ones on the other side. There is no chance with the time, space, and distance that existed between Olivia and Finn that a higher power had the biggest hand in guiding them together. Then to find out that Dan and Christine were friends while here in the physical world is nothing short of miraculous. A love story to beat all love stories. Liv's mom, Trish, and I are abundantly grateful for you, Finn. The happiness you've brought into Olivia's life is the greatest gift a parent could ask for. She has found her true best friend and soulmate in you. We want to welcome you and your parents, Alistar and Fiona, into our lives. This union has healed all our souls. God bless you both. We love you." He doesn't leave a dry eye in the room. "On a lighter note, the bar is open and we are ready to get this party started. Cheers," he jokes, eliciting a chuckle from the group.

Garrett is emceeing for this night. He doesn't want the DJ interjecting and getting all cheesy. He might spontaneously combust if he plays the "Macarena" or "Chicken Dance". His role is to play music from the very specific set of songs provided. No veering off the well-defined instructions. Finn and I are invited to the dance floor for our first dance, another surprise for Finn. We're dancing to "Into the Mystic" by Van Morrison. It was the initial song that played at his house the night he made me dinner for the first time. Then we break into "Castle on the Hill" by Ed Sheeran for the wedding party to dance to. It has special meaning to both of us. Ed Sheeran is Scottish, and the song refers to growing up with old pals and how you miss that feeling of being young and free. A perfect, upbeat tribute to our adolescence. The next few hours are packed with endless favorites, including "Small Town". As the evening is winding down, Garrett invites everyone outside to light a lantern and make a wish. *My wish is for every day with the love of my life to get better and better.*

Finn and I say our goodbyes and are driven back to the inn. He carries me over the threshold of the honeymoon suite and says, "Mrs. McDaniels, I can't wait to spend my forever with ye cause yer now mine."

CHAPTER TWENTY
(FINN)

We are off to Tulum, Mexico for our honeymoon. It's on the Yucatan Peninsula, also known as the Mexican Riviera. This is Mac and Jules' secret getaway, so it comes highly recommended. It's only a short flight from Austin. We take an early flight out to maximize beach time. I arrange for a personal driver to take us to the resort, which is an hour away. He's waiting with sign in hand as soon as we leave customs with our luggage. *Welcome Mr. & Mrs. McDaniels*. I make a pit stop in the duty-free store to purchase some Don Julio tequila. This is what the locals drink, so it must be the best. Jose, our chauffer, comes prepared with a cooler full of Corona and the honeymoon commences. The resort, Casa Bonita, Tulum, is first class. We have a private beach cottage that extends out into the ocean. It comes with its own pool so we are guaranteed privacy. The honeymoon package gives us full access to exclusive areas on the resort. We have our own butler, an assigned cabana on the beach, and something special is included daily. Things like breakfast in bed, a couple's massage, a romantic candlelight dinner on the beach, and a sunset catamaran cruise. We plan to be pampered for the next eight days. When we arrive to check-in, the bellman escorts us to our room. It is glorious. The structure is made of concrete due to the elements, but they disguise it with a Polynesian hut motif. It has two levels. The main floor offers a sprawling sun-deck with lounge chairs, an outdoor shower, kitchen, a generous fresh water swimming pool, and a ladder with direct access to the ocean. It even comes equipped with snorkel gear. Upstairs opens into one large, luxurious open space with big, fluffy, white oversized furniture and a wet bar. It has a king-sized canopy bed covered in rose petals. We see a bucket of champagne and chocolate covered strawberries next to the bed. Compliments of Garrett and Tristan. We are in awe that we get to call this home for the next week. It's beyond our expectations.

"Shall we get our suits on?" Liv asks, opening the sliding glass door onto the patio overlooking the water.

"Aye, our birthday suits," I respond, grabbing her and pulling her down on top of me on the bed.

"*Mmmm*, Mr. McDaniels. You are irresistible," she gushes.

"This place is amazing, but we may not see much of anything but the inside of this room," I joke. "We need to christen this bed, that couch, those lounge chairs, the outdoor shower, the indoor shower, bathtub, the pool, the ocean . . . shall I go on?"

"You need to shut up and kiss me," she says, and we spend the next few hours making love, followed by a much-needed nap.

We wake up and tour the grounds to see what we have in store for the next several days. The resort is beautiful, not overly crowded. The main area has an infinity pool with a swim up bar. It has restaurants on either side. One menu offers tapas, and the other is a steakhouse. There is also a traditional Mexican restaurant closer to the lobby. This is an adults only resort, so there are many honeymooners. We won't have trouble making friends. We waste no time getting in and bellying up to the bar. A few minutes into our first drink, a couple joins us and invites us to join them for a tequila shot and a round of pool volleyball. We work up an appetite and decide that steak sounds like the perfect first meal. We sit down to order steak, medium rare, and a short while later the waiter returns with meat that can only be described as hockey pucks. The steak was charcoaled to the point of no return.

"Liv, this is unacceptable. I will not allow my new bride's first meal being married to a chef be this intolerable. I have to rectify this," I say as I stand from the table.

"Finn, sit down. What are you doing?" she asks in a concerned tone.

"Don't worry, I'm not going to cause a scene, but I am going to introduce myself to the hombres in the kitchen and give them a free lesson in steak grilling," he jokes.

"Finn McDaniels, sit down," she demands, trying to stop me as I charge, uninvited, toward the kitchen.

"It's fine . . . just watch," I say with her in tow.

Much to my surprise, *Delectable* must have been a very popular show in Mexico because the cooks in the kitchen recognize me and begin to shout "*Concinero, Concinero.*"

"Oh my God, what are they saying? *Get out??*" she inquires.

"They are chanting *chef* in Spanish. They must recognize me from the show."

"Now *that's* funny."

"And buckle up, yer bout to learn something new about me," I tease.

"Oh yeah, what's that?"

"Watch this," I claim as I begin to speak. "Buena noches caballeros, como estas?"

"No habla," the head cook, Julio, responds, laughing. "Just kidding. We speak English, and may I say, Chef McDaniels, it is an honor to meet you. We all watched your show," he says.

"Aye, brilliant. This is my new wife, Olivia. We are here for the next week. We love yer resort, but, listen, we ordered steak and I'm not sure if maybe the waiter wrote it down wrong, but it came out well done. We asked for medium rare. No big deal, but I was wondering if ye would mind if I helped to grill up a couple more. Ye know, force of habit," I joke.

"Of course. Mi casa es tu casa," he says as he makes way for me to take charge. "Please, cook for your beautiful wife. I could learn a thing or two from you."

I cook them to perfection then Liv and I head back out to our table to enjoy our meal.

"I didn't know you spoke Spanish," she says. "And not to be cocky, but other than chef, I understood all of that."

"Ye work in enough kitchens, you pick up on languages," I joke.

"I hope this meat doesn't kill us. I'm sure their regulations are much less restrictive than ours, which may be why they cooked the shit out of them," she comments. "So, I blame *you* for any explosive diarrhea."

We polish off our bottle of wine with dinner and call it an early night.

As we arrive back to the room, I say, "We haven't been in the ocean yet. Let's skinny dip."

"I don't do the ocean at night. I have to be able to see underneath me with the sharks and all."

"I'm yer husband. I'll protect ye," I assure.

"Oh yeah, how?" she asks.

"I'll shout, 'she tastes like chicken' then run for help," I joke.

"Nice, but let's stick with the pool when it's not daylight," she responds.

We are up and out early. Today we are doing an all-day trip to tour the Mayan Ruins, which are right up my alley. Reminds me of all the old architecture in Scotland. It also includes snorkeling in the underground sea caves. They call them *cenotes*. Mac raved about it. I fill a flask with tequila, and we are off. We meet some other great couples in the group. They feed us lunch they call chicken and I would call iguana, but I don't want to alarm Liv. I keep handing off the flask to keep her with a healthy buzz, so she doesn't notice some of the questionable options.

Tonight, we have our candlelight dinner on the beach. The staff is aware of our presence after my impromptu kitchen visit last night. Since then, service has been terrific. The setting is majestic. We arrive just before sunset and order a bottle of champagne when a mariachi band approaches and serenades Liv to "I Just Called to Say I Love You" by Lionel Ritchie. As I watch Liv, streams of tears fall down her cheeks, overcome with emotion.

"I still can't believe I'm your wife," Liv gushes. "The last two years have been nothing short of a whirlwind and I have to be honest: I don't mean this in a bad way, but this is not at *all* what I expected."

"What do you mean?" I ask.

"I don't know. I mean, let's use the way you met and fell in love with Christine as an example. You were young. You had a friend in common and it happened naturally; it was somewhat effortless. I always figured I would end up being set up with a friend or meet someone through work or a client. I wasn't expecting you *at all* and then you were just here. I'm sure you can agree it hasn't been the fairytale romance most people hope for, or at least not the one I dreamed about. It's messier than I expected. This is not coming out the way I mean it. This is so much *more* than what I ever dreamt of. We've already been through a lifetime together. The pain we both went through before we even met. The stars that had to align for us to find each other. Then being forced to separate, Owen getting sick, almost losing you to a terrorist attack, and then the whole Mac drama. It's been an insanely bumpy ride."

"Aye, that's true," I respond.

"I cannot imagine going through it with anyone else. I wouldn't have survived any of it without you. You are my best friend, my soulmate, *my everything*, Finn McDaniels. I don't know if I tell you that enough. You are the only one who's been able to repair the giant hole in my heart. Because of you, I know what true happiness is. I treasure you," she says, reaching over the table for a lingering kiss.

"Aye. Yer pretty remarkable yerself. And on that note, I think I need to feed ye tequila all day, every day," I joke.

We finish our surf and turf just as the sun is setting.

"I have a surprise for ye." I reach under the table to grab the wishing paper and a lighter. I grab her hand and move closer to the water.

"I had this amazing speech planned then ye went and ruined it at dinner." I laugh. "Naw, but, really, our wedding day went by in a flash and we never had our memorable moment, so I want to recreate it here tonight. I bought this wishing paper. We write down our wishes then crumple up the paper, light it on fire, and the wind will disperse the ashes into the air. Let's each write down three wishes. Two for us and one for Christine and Dan," I suggest.

"You are so thoughtful, I love you. Sounds perfect," she says, kissing me.

I hand her the paper and a pen and turn around so she can use my back to write her wishes. I follow suit and then turn around to face her.

"Okay, you first," I say to her.

"My first wish is for us to be blessed with a long, happy, successful life together, whatever that entails. My second wish is for our hardships to keep us loyal, determined, and humble. My third wish is for Dan and Christine to always watch over us, keep us safe, and be with us," she says. "Your turn."

"Wow. Those are beautiful." I lean in for a sweet kiss. "My first wish is for you to be as in love with me, as you are today, all the days of my life. My second wish is for us to be blessed with a beautiful family, whatever that looks like. My third wish is for Christine and Dan to be able to stay with us and show us signs of their love forever." We light the papers on fire and send them up into the sky.

#

The week is going by so fast, so we decide to stay at the resort and relax all day. We have a sunset cocktail catamaran cruise scheduled for this evening. We start with a swim in the ocean off the balcony of our room then head into the beach and settle into our cabana for the day. We're alternating between regular and frozen fruit margaritas. It's in the low nineties today with no breeze, so we're in the water quite a bit. The water is crystal blue and not too choppy. Perfect. By mid-afternoon, we're working on a really good buzz and start adding a tequila shot every few drinks.

"Liv, check out this bee. I think he's drunk from hanging around all the sugary drinks. Little does he know they are full of tequila. He's trying to land on me but keeps getting stuck in my leg hair. He's not moving fast enough so is like *oh my god, I'm trapped in a dense forest, heeeeeeeeelp*!" I joke.

"Finn, I don't feel so good. I think I need to go back to the room," she says, sounding woozy.

"Okay, let me help ye." I help her out of the lounge chair. She starts walking toward the cottage when I notice her feet. They are full of sand, and by full of sand, I mean caked on to her mid-calf like ski boots. I have to convince her to go over to the outdoor shower to rinse off before our bed is a giant sandbox. I get her back to the room and in bed, but it is now crystal clear that I will be taking a romantic catamaran cruise all by my lonesome.

Today is our last day in paradise, and Liv is down for the count, sicker than a dog. She hasn't surfaced all day and is not too pleased with me either. She thinks I'm the enabler and should have cut her off sooner. I give her some space and make my last rounds on the resort. It's been such a wonderful trip. I hate to end it on a sour note. I need to convince her it's Montezuma's revenge and not the tequila.

CHAPTER TWENTY-ONE
(OLIVIA)

It takes every ounce of Finn's energy to pull himself out of bed.

"I never want this to end. I just want to lay here with ye forever. Can't we stop time?" he asks.

"I know. I don't know how I will survive the next ten hours without you," I say, following him into the bathroom, trying to jump start our first day back in Palm Springs. The last couple weeks have been nothing short of extraordinary. I don't want it to be over. It's been nice to be disconnected from our phones and only focus on each other.

I check my phone after Finn leaves for the restaurant. I already have three texts from Garrett.

"Morning, sweetie. I've been dying to talk to you. How was the honeymoon?" Garrett asks.

"It was perfect. We had so much fun," I say.

"What was the resort like?"

"It was on the smallish side, kind of quiet but perfect for us. It was heaven."

"Would you guys go back?" he asks.

"For sure. The food wasn't that spectacular, but I kept my expectations low because I am married to a world-renowned chef. It was nice for Finn to be waited on hand and foot for a week. He never gets to relax and is always in the kitchen. They had a half dozen restaurants, so we typically had brunch then dinner. One night I didn't actually make it to dinner," I say.

"Why, what happened?" he asks.

"Tommy Tequila," I joke.

"Oh no," he says.

"Yeah, we got cocky and started drinking shots. Let's just say it didn't end well. I didn't leave the room the entire next day I was so hungover. I sent Finn to have a massage, and he met some other guys traveling that kept him entertained. I have to be honest, though; I haven't been feeling great since. Probably Montezuma's revenge," I mention.

"Well, can you meet me for lunch? I'm dying to dish on the wedding," he asks.

"Sure, I'll come by the store around eleven thirty and we can go grab something."

"Sounds good. See you soon."

As soon as we hang up, it dawns on me. I have no idea when my last period was. It's been one thing after another and with all the wedding activities, I didn't even pay attention. I text Garrett.

OLIVIA: Change of plans. Meet me at the house. Explain later.

GARRETT: *Okay, want me to bring lunch.*

OLIVIA: No, I have to run out. I'll pick something up.

I take a shower and go to the drugstore to pick up a pregnancy test. Make that three pregnancy tests. I stop at the Italian deli in the same shopping center and pick up some sandwiches and a salad. By the time I get home, Garrett is waiting in the driveway.

"What's up?" he asks, and I pull the test out of my bag. "Oh my God, no," he reacts. "You've been married for fourteen seconds. You're *already* pregnant?"

"I don't know yet, silly. Hence the tests and multiple ones, so I can know for sure," I say, leading him through the garage into the house. "You start getting the lunch ready, and I will go start one of these," I say, waving the box.

"Okay, but what if you are pregnant? Shouldn't Finn know before me?" he inquires as he walks toward the cabinets to grab plates.

"You're kidding, right?" I shout from the bathroom.

"No, why?"

"Didn't he call you to pick out my engagement ring while I was barely able to lift my head off my pillow, and ask you to keep it a secret from me for three weeks?" I declare.

"Ohhhhh, right."

"I think it's my turn for a little element of surprise if I am pregnant."

"Touche," he replies. "Hurry up and wash those hands under scalding hot water before you come to the table."

"I took care of my hygiene. You need not worry," I say, grabbing the salt and pepper off the countertop on my way to the table.

"How long does it take?" he asks.

"Five minutes. I set the alarm on my phone," I respond, about to sit down. "Oh, who are we kidding; let's go watch it." I grab his hand, dragging him into the bathroom and see the bright pink line staring us in the face.

"You are *frickin'* pregnant. I cannot believe it. So much for you traveling the world and enjoying coupledom before getting knocked up," he announces.

"Supportive as always. This *wasn't* planned. Oh my God, I cannot believe this." I pick up the stick and shake it to see if maybe it malfunctioned. I shove him out and slam the door to take the other two to be triple positive this is really happening.

"I mean, birth control 101, aren't you on the pill?" he asks through the door.

"Yes, but I guess maybe I've missed a couple here and there with all of our traveling. I didn't really think about it," I respond. "I can't believe it. It's wrong. It's gotta be wrong, right?"

"How do you think Finn is going to react?" he inquires.

"I'm assuming he will be thrilled. I know he and Christine tried to have kids. We never really talked about how soon we wanted to have kids, but we want two, at least," I reply.

"Let's pray it's *not* twins. *Wait*, Jane has twins; isn't it hereditary or something?" he comments.

"Don't even go there. One will be plenty." I glance down to see the other two tests glowing pink.

"Holy shit. I am pregnant," I reveal, opening the door and showing him all three positive results as I pace back and forth with nervous energy.

"How are you going to tell him?"

"I haven't gotten that far. He's not working late tonight, so maybe I'll surprise him by making dinner and do something clever with Frank."

"Good luck, sweetie. I'm out," he says as he walks out the garage door back to his car.

#

I feel nauseous suddenly. It almost feels like I might have a panic attack. The first thing that pops into my head is this baby has to eventually come out of me. Oh my God. *Through my vagina.* Okay, settle down, settle down. Take some deep breaths. This will be fine. You can do this. I find a bench to sit on in the grocery store to calm down. I'm here to pick up ingredients. I'm making a grilled pork tenderloin with a molasses and soy crust, asparagus, and garlic mashed potatoes.

OLIVIA: Hi love. What time will you be home tonight?

FINN: I should be home by 8 p.m. at the latest.

OLIVIA: Ok, text me if anything changes. Love you!

FINN: Will do. XO.

I start getting ingredients together around six thirty and start the grill at seven when I get a text.

FINN: On my way now. See you soon. XO.

I put a cute outfit on and primp a bit. After all, this is big news. I want Finn to remember what I look like the moment I tell him he's going to be a daddy. I get the note ready for Frank and wait for him to arrive.

"Wifey?" he calls out as he comes through the front door.

"I'm in the kitchen," I answer as he turns the corner.

"Well, well, well what is goin' on in here?" he asks, wrapping his arms around me and pulling me in for a kiss.

"I thought I'd surprise you and make you dinner for a change. I figured you got used to not cooking while we were in Mexico." I hand him a glass of red wine.

"I could get used to this. What are you making? Smells delicious." He leans over me to get a closer look.

"Pork tenderloin, asparagus, and garlic mashed potatoes."

"I'm impressed, Liv," he says as he bends down to give Frank some love.

"Go sit down. I have to finish cutting the meat. It's been resting for a few minutes."

"If I didn't know better, I'd say you were a professional," he jokes.

"The benefits of sleeping with a chef. Comes with the territory."

"Let's hurry up and get to dessert," he says as he rubs my ass while I deliver the food to the table. I make one last trip over to the stove area and grab the envelope to give to Frank. I put it in his mouth and give him the hand signal telling him to stay.

"Shall we?" I say as I approach the table, gesturing to sit down. "Oh wait, I forgot one thing . . . Frank, come here, boy." Frank approaches, wagging his tail with the envelope in his mouth.

"Whaddya got there, bud?" Finn asks, bending down to retrieve the envelope from Frank. He opens it and reads it out loud. "*Mommy says I'm going to be a big brother. Do you want a boy or a girl?*" He looks up at me in disbelief. "A baby? Really, Liv?" he asks, welling up with tears. I nod in response and embrace him.

He's collecting his thoughts, trying to absorb what he just heard. "This is *beyond* brilliant . . . I'm going to be a da."

www.ddmarx.com

CPSIA information can be obtained
at www.ICGtesting.com
Printed in the USA
LVOW13s1127250817
546296LV00003B/3/P